HE WAS HERE

Published by Anthony Malloy

contact@anthonymalloyauthor.com

First Edition 2026

Cover design by Amina N.

Editing by Paige Lawson

Formatting by Anthony Malloy

ISBN: 979-8-9995993-6-0 (Paperback)

ISBN: 979-8-9995993-7-7 (Hardcover)

ISBN: 979-8-9995993-8-4 (eBook)

For Papaw,
Mama Peach,
and Dad.

May you Rest In Peace.

We are each our own devil, and we make this world
our hell.

— OSCAR WILDE

He Was Here

A NOVEL

ANTHONY MALLOY

CHAPTER
ONE

NIKO

The porch light was still on.

It buzzed faintly in the summer heat, casting a sickly yellow glow over the front steps—the same porch where Tony Russo once stood and told me to get my shit together or lose the badge. He always left that light on, said it helped guide people home.

Now it just made everything look more haunted.

DJ stood by the gate, arms crossed, jaw clenched. He didn't wave me over. Didn't say a word. Just nodded once. Slow. The kind of nod that says, Don't go in there.

He looked the same as always: solid, broad, his buzz cut streaked with gray that complimented his soft caramel skin tone. His shirt was wrinkled, badge clipped low on his belt since he couldn't be bothered with appearances. He had this permanent tiredness in his eyes, the kind that came from too many years and too many dead kids. The old Marine tattoo on his forearm peeked out from under his rolled-up sleeve. I'd seen that ink for most of my career. I never noticed how much older it looked until tonight.

Darius "DJ" Jacks. My current partner. My dad's old partner. My last line of defense, whether I deserved one or not.

I passed him without a word.

The front door creaked open without resistance. Inside, the house was still. No movement. No sounds. Just the steady tick of that cheap wall clock Dad never got around to replacing.

He'd lived alone since Mom passed. Kept the place spotless. Still had that cop precision, even in retirement. Everything in its place.

The scent hit me next, thick, sharp, and metallic. Blood. Not dried. Not old.

Fresh.

I stepped inside carefully, one foot after the other, past the coat rack, past the end table with the chipped photo frame of me and him at my academy graduation.

Two generations of detectives.

Now one of us was a crime scene.

Down the hallway. Into the kitchen.

And there he was.

Tony Russo, face-up on the tile. Blood pooled around his head, already darkening at the edges. His body was twisted, one arm sprawled across the floor, the other tucked underneath him like he'd tried to shield something.

His badge lay near his fingers. Bent. Dented. As if someone had stepped on it.

I couldn't move. Couldn't breathe. My legs locked while my hands trembled in my jacket pockets.

He looked smaller than I remembered. Shrunken. Fragile. This wasn't the man who raised me, who commanded precincts without raising his voice. This was a body. A slab.

I didn't realize I was on my knees until I felt the cold seeping through my jeans.

DJ's boots appeared in my peripheral. He stayed back, silent, knowing the moment would break if he said too much.

"I told them to wait," he murmured. "Told 'em you should be first in."

I couldn't answer. My throat was a dry knot.

"There's something else," he said. "We found him like this."

I looked up.

DJ nodded toward the body.

I followed his gaze and the world fractured.

Not a clean shatter—more like bone splintering under pressure.

My father's eyes were gone. Two gaping red voids where they used to be. His ears were torn, shredded at the edges. His mouth was open slightly, a ragged hole where his tongue had been.

I jerked backward.

"What the fuck..." I whispered, though it came out like a wheeze.

DJ crouched beside me, his face harder than I'd ever seen it. "Medical examiner hasn't touched him yet. But this was deliberate."

Speak no evil.

See no evil.

Hear no evil.

The phrase looped in my brain like static.

He was here.

This was a message.

A message carved into my father's fucking face.

I reached out a shaking hand but stopped halfway—afraid to touch him.

His badge, dented and broke, stared back at me like an accusation.

A single breath scraped out of my lungs. "Who would—"

But the question never finished.

My brain answered before I could form the words.

Dante.

His style. His signature. His cruelty.

I stood slowly, my knees buckling. My chest burned because my lungs forgot how to work.

I stared at DJ.

He stared back.

My voice cracked. "It was fucking Dante. This is how he kills. I bet Dad was finally onto him. He should've just told me."

Then I turned and walked out of the house, into the dark—past the porch light, still buzzing, still shining.

Still waiting for someone to come home.

The drive home was a blur of red lights and tunnel vision.

I couldn't feel my hands on the wheel. Couldn't feel much of anything, really. Just that high-pitched static behind my eyes.

It wasn't until I pulled into the driveway that the shaking started.

I cut the engine and sat there in the dark, gripping the steering wheel as if it was the only thing holding me together. The porch light at our place was off, Rose always hated the bugs, but the house still looked warm. Alive.

I didn't move.

Not until the sob hit.

Not quiet. Not controlled. The kind that comes from the gut. Ugly, gasping, teeth-clenched, the kind of sound you make when something rips straight through you.

I slammed my fists into the wheel again and again until the horn blared and the tears blurred everything.

"Fuck," I growled, choking on it.

Then a hand touched my arm.

I flinched so hard I hit my head on the ceiling.

"Hey. It's me," she said softly.

Rose. A wife I don't deserve. Barefoot in the driveway, wrapped in a faded hoodie and pajama pants, her chestnut hair tied in a messy bun, wisps escaping at the edges. Her soft green eyes blinked up at me, tired but full of that quiet strength she always carried. A faded tattoo peeked from her forearm: *Always*.

She opened the car door and crouched beside me, her hand sliding to my knee.

"Baby," she whispered. "What happened?"

I couldn't speak at first. The words felt too big. Too sharp.

But then I looked at her, really looked at her, and the truth just broke loose.

"It's my dad. He's dead," I said.

She froze.

I wiped my face with the back of my sleeve. "Murdered. The way they found him, the way he was staged. Eyes gone. Ears torn. Tongue cut out."

Her hand tightened on my leg.

"That's not some random act of rage. That's someone sending a message." I looked at her. "That's Dante."

She didn't argue. Didn't flinch.

But her breath hitched once.

"Have they confirmed that?" she asked.

"Not yet. But I know it. I've seen this before."

"In your dad's old files?"

I nodded.

She stood up slowly, tugging on my arm. "Come inside. You're freezing."

"I don't want to sleep."

"I didn't say sleep."

She led me toward the house, one hand still gripping mine.

As the door closed behind us, I looked over my shoulder.

The night felt too quiet.

Like something, or someone, was listening.

CHAPTER
TWO

NIKO

I couldn't sleep.

The clock read 4:11 AM, and I'd been staring at the ceiling so long I'd memorized the cracks in the paint. Rose had passed out hours ago, curled against my back, one arm flung across my waist to keep me grounded.

I slipped out of bed without waking her and padded barefoot into the kitchen. The floorboards creaked under my weight, and the silence buzzed louder than the fridge.

I made coffee, because it was the only ritual that made sense.

I caught my reflection in the microwave door, unshaven, dark circles under my eyes, hair a mess from the drive. Thirty-two and I looked older. Grief did that.

Then I sat at the table and pulled out the folder DJ had dropped off.

Funeral arrangements. Press coordination. Burial options. Badge ceremony protocols.

All of it written in cold, efficient type. My father's death turned into a checklist.

I flipped past the forms until I hit the photo they'd used for the internal memo, Tony at a retirement party three years ago. He was smiling. Tight, like he didn't want to. His dress blues still fit back then. His hand rested on my shoulder.

He looked proud. But he always did in photos. That was the trick with him. He made it look effortless even when it wasn't.

I rubbed my eyes and leaned back in the chair.

And just like that, I was twenty-four again.

Standing in his office during my first week on the job, still green enough to think I could impress him.

"You're not here to be my son," he said, voice low but sharp. "You're here to be a cop. That means no favors. No special treatment."

"I didn't ask for—"

"You didn't have to." He set down the file he was reading and looked at me. Really looked.

"I've seen a lot of guys lose their edge trying to live up to their old man. You screw up? I'll bury you just like anyone else on this floor. You get that?"

I swallowed. "Yeah."

"You want to make me proud?" he asked. "Don't. Just do the fucking job."

That was our version of love.

No hugs. No I'm proud of you. Just pressure. Expectation. The unspoken bond of shared silence and clipped approval.

And it worked. At least for a while.

Until the department retired him early. Until the case with Dante cracked him wide open. Until he became that guy, the old cop calling in tips no one wanted, handing out theories like flyers no one asked for.

I kept telling myself he was just grieving, that he didn't know how to stop being useful.

But deep down, I think he knew it was coming. That Dante would find him again.

And now I was the one left picking through the wreckage.

I turned over the last page in the file and stared at the form asking next of kin to sign off on cremation or burial.

My hand hovered over the pen.

It shook.

The pen never touched the paper. I just sat there, hand suspended, fingers twitching like they couldn't decide whether to sign or snap in half.

I exhaled, long and shaky, and closed the folder halfway.

For a second, I let myself believe I could be done for the night—that I could just... stop.

My hands didn't get the message. They kept flipping pages even while my brain begged for quiet.

And then I saw it.

Tucked behind the standard forms, paper-clipped to the coroner's report.

Dante Crowe.

My stomach dropped.

I should've closed the folder. Walked away. Woken Rose.

Instead, I sat perfectly still, like the paper had teeth and moving too fast might make it bite.

Printed in clean type at the top of an old case summary, one I hadn't seen in years. Cold case. Unresolved. Buried by time and politics and collective willful forgetting.

But not by my father.

The sight of that name punched me in the chest.

I pulled the document free and spread it flat across the table. The edges were worn; it had been folded and refolded too many times. Tony's handwriting covered the margins.

> *Eyes. Ears. Tongue. Always the same.*
> *Always clean.*
> *This isn't rage. This is ritual.*
> *Crowe = symbol, not just a man.*

Below the notes was a photocopied mugshot. Not from an arrest, more like a background file. Maybe a driver's license. He looked younger then, hair shaved close, hollow eyes, something almost smug in the way he didn't smile.

I stared at the picture until it blurred.

Dante wasn't a ghost. Not to my father.

Tony had been chasing him for years, long after the department moved on, long after the cases went cold. He'd called it a pattern, said there was a message in the mutilation.

Speak no evil. See no evil. Hear no evil.

I used to tell him he was reaching.

Now I wasn't so sure.

The staging in our kitchen matched every detail.

And here I was, exhausted, shaking, knowing damn well I needed rest.

Obsession wasn't sneaking up on me. I was already letting it in.

My father didn't just die.

He was silenced.

CHAPTER
THREE

NIKO

The sun wasn't up yet, but I was already dressed.

Dark jeans. Plain black shirt. Badge clipped at the hip. Not for show, for access.

The Dante file sat open on the table, surrounded by old post-its and crime scene photos my father had hoarded. Some were stained. Others were barely legible. He'd traced patterns across them like a madman, circles around symbols and strings of red ink connecting victims no one had ever linked.

I saw it now. All of it.

The precision. The staging. The signature.

And the name underneath it all: **Dante Crowe.**

I picked up my phone and sent the name to DJ with one line beneath it.

"I'm going after him."

I didn't wait for a reply.

"Seriously?" Rose's voice came from behind me.

I turned.

She stood in the kitchen doorway in a hoodie and sleep shorts, arms crossed, hair wild with sleep. No makeup. No softness in her expression.

"You're not going to wait for the department to assign you to the case?" she asked.

I slipped the holster over my shoulder. "I don't care."

"And what? You think you're just going to find him? Alone?"

"I think if I wait for them, he'll be gone again. Just like he always is."

She stepped forward, her voice low and tight. "You're not ready for this. You just buried your dad."

"I haven't even scheduled the funeral."

That stopped her.

I closed the folder and stuffed it into my bag.

"Don't do this," she said. "Not like this. Not now."

I could hear it in her voice, the fear buried under the concern. The edge she didn't want me to hear.

"You think I'm wrong?" I asked gently.

"I think you're hurting. I think you're seeing things you want to see."

I walked to her. Rested my forehead against hers for a moment and closed my eyes. Her hands slid to the back of my neck, right where my dark hair was starting to curl.

"You weren't there," I said softly. "You didn't see what he did to him."

She didn't answer.

I stepped back and grabbed my keys.

"I'll call you when I have something. I love you, babe."

"Niko."

The door shut behind me before she could finish.

The city slid past in a blur: traffic lights, wet pavement, cigarette butts glowing in gutters from the night before.

I gripped the wheel hard enough to hurt. The folder sat open in the passenger seat, pages rustling every time I turned. My eyes kept flicking to the photo clipped to the front.

Dante Crowe.

He stared back like he knew I was coming.

My phone buzzed. DJ.

I hesitated, then answered with a curt, "Yeah?"

"Where the hell are you?" His voice was fast and tense. "Please tell me you're not doing what I think you're doing."

"I'm following a lead."

"You're not on the case, Niko."

"Neither were any of the victims, DJ."

A beat of silence.

"I know you're grieving," he said, voice softer now. "But you can't go at this alone."

DJ exhaled, a frustrated, tired sound.

"You're too close to this. You can't see straight. You need backup. Or at least me."

"I'm not waiting for red tape, DJ. I'm not letting him disappear again."

Another silence, longer this time. I didn't need backup. I needed movement.

Then he said, "I might know where he is."

I gritted my teeth. "Then stop wasting time."

"I didn't say it was solid. Just a whisper. Someone says

they saw him near the old plant at the bottom of Price Hill. No cameras. Half the building's condemned."

I flipped my turn signal. "Text me the address."

"Niko."

"I'll be fine."

"No, you won't. That's what scares me."

I didn't answer.

"You find him," DJ said slowly, "you don't go in. You call me. You wait."

I hung up without replying.

Because we both knew I wasn't going to wait.

The plant sat like a rotting carcass on the edge of Price Hill, rusted fencing, busted windows, and a sagging metal sign that still read *Muir Manufacturing Co.* in half-peeled lettering.

No lights. No sound. Just the hum of nearby power lines and the soft crunch of gravel under my boots as I stepped through the fence break.

I moved slow, hand on my holster, breath steady.

The place smelled like wet metal and piss. Old machines sat frozen inside, cloaked in dust. I didn't know what I was expecting: a candlelit altar, fresh blood, a welcome mat?

What I found was worse.

Movement.

Just beyond a broken support beam, near one of the side exits, I caught a figure slipping out the door. Tall. Lean. Hooded.

He didn't run. He didn't look back.

He walked, calm as hell, like he had all the time in the world.

My pulse spiked.

"Hey!" I barked.

He kept walking.

I ran.

I burst through the exit just in time to see him reach a black sedan idling by the loading dock. The brake lights flared.

The driver's side door opened.

And for one brief second, he turned his head, just enough for the streetlight to catch his profile.

It was him.

Even after all these years, I knew that face.

Dante. Fucking. Crowe.

I sprinted.

"Not this time," I muttered.

The car peeled away in a screech of tires and exhaust. I dove into mine, jammed the key in the ignition, and shot out of the lot after him, high beams on, engine howling.

He wanted to run?

Let him.

I was ready to chase.

CHAPTER
FOUR

NIKO

The tires screamed as I took the first turn too fast.

Downtown Cincinnati blurred past, steel and brick and wet neon. The streets were still half asleep, fog curling up from manholes like the city was trying to exhale.

Dante's black sedan weaved through traffic ahead, always just far enough to stay out of reach. Always just fast enough to taunt me.

I gunned the engine.

He took a sharp left onto Vine, skidding through a red light. Horns blared as other cars slammed their brakes. I followed without thinking.

A part of me knew this wasn't strategy, it was grief with its foot on the gas.

My body was reacting faster than my mind. Instinct had taken the wheel and wasn't planning to give it back.

He cut through a narrow side street, tires kicking up water from last night's rain. Trash cans toppled. A dog barked somewhere in the distance, startled by the violence of it.

I stayed close. Closer than he expected.

He didn't know I'd driven these streets since I was seventeen. Didn't know I'd once chased a meth head through this exact alley in a beat-up cruiser with half a bumper.

Didn't know I'd already decided I wasn't letting him vanish again.

My chest tightened, a hot, nauseating squeeze that had nothing to do with speed.

If I lost him now, the image of my dad on that kitchen floor would never leave my mind. I couldn't live with that.

We blasted out onto Race Street, lights overhead strobing across the windshield like a warning. He clipped the side mirror of a parked SUV but kept going. I dodged it by inches, tires shrieking.

The speedometer tipped past ninety.

I could barely hear myself think over the roar of the engine and the wind through my cracked window, but my mind kept whispering the same thing:

It's him. It's really him.

He took another turn, almost missed it, almost clipped the curb.

That hesitation?

That was fear.

I could feel it.

And for a split second, beneath the fury, something colder slipped in—the terrifying thought that if this ended badly, Rose would be the one getting a knock on the door next.

I slammed the wheel left, tires fishtailing as I followed him toward the overpass, the one that led out of the downtown grid and into the old industrial sector.

His brake lights flickered.

He was about to do something stupid.

So was I.

He swerved onto the overpass, tires shrieking on the slick asphalt. I stayed on him, less than two car lengths behind now. Close enough to see his license plate, close enough to taste the fucking air he was kicking up.

He jerked left, then right, trying to shake me.

But it didn't work.

We barreled down the curve as the road narrowed, construction barriers on both sides, half-finished repairs choking the lane.

Dante's car clipped one. Sparks flew.

He overcorrected.

Too fast. Too sharp.

His back tire hit a patch of standing water and spun.

I saw the back end swing wide.

I hit the brakes hard, but it was too late.

My car slammed into his.

Metal screamed.

Glass exploded.

The world tilted.

I felt weightlessness, the kind that means something is about to go very, very wrong.

Then the impact.

I tasted blood. Saw the windshield crack like ice under a boot.

Something in my neck snapped sideways. My head

slammed against the doorframe. Lights burst behind my eyes.

Then nothing.

Somewhere in the wreckage of sound and metal, I heard my father's voice.

Or maybe it was just fear pretending to be memory.

Just a high-pitched tone in the dark.

And silence.

FIVE

NIKO

Beeping.

That was the first thing.

Not voices. Not light. Not even pain.

Just the steady, insistent beep of something trying to convince me I was still alive.

I opened my eyes slowly. Regretted it immediately.

Fluorescent lights above me. Pale green walls. A thin blanket over my chest. My right arm strapped with wires. An IV pumping cold into my veins.

Hospital.

The room was too quiet. No Rose. No DJ.

Just antiseptic air and the distant sound of a hallway machine rolling past.

I tried to sit up.

The pain was a blade slicing through my ribs.

"Easy," a voice said.

I turned my head, slower this time.

A doctor stood at the edge of the bed, tablet in hand,

wearing that careful expression they give you right before bad news. Mid-forties, brown skin, shaved head, wireframe glasses. Calm, clinical, unreadable.

"How long...?" My voice cracked.

"You've been unconscious for thirty-six hours," he said. "You had a concussion, mild internal bleeding, two fractured ribs, and a deep laceration near your temple. You're lucky to be alive."

I blinked.

"Car accident," I muttered.

He nodded.

"I need to talk to someone," I said, trying to push myself upright again.

He set a hand on my shoulder. "Detective Russo, I need you to be patient. You experienced significant head trauma. We need to assess your memory first."

"I remember the crash."

"What else?"

I hesitated.

Flashes.

Rain. Tires. Brake lights.

A face in the dark.

Dante.

"I was chasing someone," I said.

He gave me the same neutral nod.

"I remember him."

"You were found alone," he said gently. "The other vehicle was gone by the time responders arrived."

I stared at him.

"That's impossible."

"There were no other skid marks. No signs of impact

beyond your vehicle." He paused.

"No. No, that—that's wrong." My voice shook. "I didn't imagine a whole fucking car. I didn't crash myself into nothing."

"I'm not saying you're wrong. I'm saying we need to be thorough."

I closed my eyes.

The room tilted on its axis. If the crash was real, why didn't the aftermath match? Why didn't the evidence match? Every question made my head throb harder, like my own brain didn't trust me.

No. I saw him. I know I did.

My pulse thudded in my ears.

"Is anyone else here?" I asked.

"Your wife's in the waiting room. And a colleague... Darius Jacks?"

"DJ," I muttered.

"They'll be in shortly. We're monitoring your vitals for another few hours first."

He tapped the tablet. "If you remember anything else, let me know. Even fragments can help."

He turned to leave.

"Doctor," I said.

He paused.

"There was another car."

He didn't answer. Just nodded again, polite and noncommittal, and walked out.

The second the door shut, I stared at the ceiling and whispered the name like a prayer.

"Dante."

The door opened a few minutes later.

Rose walked in first, holding something pressed to her chest. Her eyes were rimmed red, hair pulled back in a loose ponytail that made her look younger. Exhausted. Hollow.

She hesitated for half a second, like she didn't know whether to rush to me or keep her distance.

Then she crossed the room and sat on the edge of the bed.

"I thought you were fucking dead," she whispered.

I didn't know what to say to that.

She reached into her bag and pulled out a framed photo.

It was old. Tony and me standing in front of his cruiser. I was probably twelve. Scrawny. Gap-toothed. Grinning like an idiot while he pretended not to smile.

He'd kept it on his desk for years.

I looked at it too long.

Something inside cracked.

I covered my face with both hands and let the sound out, low and guttural and broken. Like it didn't belong to me.

Rose pulled me into her arms and didn't say anything.

Just held me while my body shook and the grief spilled out of me like something toxic.

When it finally stopped, DJ was standing in the doorway. Silent.

He looked older under these lights, late forties, maybe fifty, shoulders still broad but carrying years instead of muscle.

He waited until Rose let go, then stepped inside and closed the door behind him.

"I'm glad you're awake," he said.

I wiped my eyes and tried to sit up straighter. "I'm sorry to both of you. I should've listened."

DJ nodded once. "No. Don't fucking do that. You're a damn good detective, and because I knew you were stubborn, I came after you. I finished the job, Niko. I caught Dante."

My chest clenched. "What?"

"I was maybe three blocks behind you when the call came in. You'd already crashed. But I kept going."

I stared at him.

"Found the sedan dumped in the warehouse district. Ran the plates. Found the bastard trying to torch evidence behind an old freight depot."

I exhaled slowly.

"Dante Crowe is in custody," DJ said. "Right now. Solitary. Under watch."

I let that sit for a moment.

It didn't feel real.

"I can't believe it. I was just chasing him. You're sure it was him?" I asked.

"Oh yeah." DJ's jaw flexed. "He didn't even run. Just smiled."

I blinked. "Smiled?"

"Like he'd been waiting for it."

The silence stretched.

"You did it," Rose whispered. "You got your fucking justice. Almost at the cost of your life."

But it didn't feel like justice.

It felt like something else.

Like the beginning of something worse.

CHAPTER
SIX
NIKO

The lights didn't feel so bright anymore.

I could breathe without the pain doubling me over, and the pounding in my skull had faded to something dull and manageable.

Still, when the doctor returned the next morning, tablet in hand and expression unreadable, I felt my whole body tense.

"Well," he said, scanning the screen, "you're making a faster recovery than expected. No internal swelling. Vitals are strong. Coordination's improving."

I nodded slowly.

"You're not cleared to go just yet," he added. "But assuming tonight passes without incident, we'll discharge you tomorrow on light duty."

That landed with more weight than I expected.

Light duty. I hadn't been benched in over a decade.

The doctor tapped a new screen open.

"We do need to talk about something," he said. "Your

MRI showed no major complications, but with trauma like this, particularly to the frontal lobe, there's always a possibility of lingering effects. Traumatic Brain Injury, also known as TBI."

I raised an eyebrow. "What kind of effects?"

"Memory gaps. Mood swings. Difficulty with impulse control. Nightmares. Hallucinations, in rare cases."

He didn't say violence. But it hung in the air between us anyway.

"You've been lucid," he added quickly. "Oriented. No signs of serious damage. But if you experience confusion, blackouts, personality shifts..."

"I'll call it in," I said.

He nodded. "We just want you aware. Most patients never notice anything. But it's better to be honest about what could happen."

A faint chill crawled up the nape of my neck. The room suddenly felt too small, like all the air had shifted half an inch to the left and I hadn't moved with it.

He paused. "Your wife mentioned you haven't been sleeping."

I shrugged. "Never been great at it."

"You should try tonight," he said. "Deep rest helps the brain knit itself back together."

As he left, I stared at the IV line in my arm and tried not to think about the words "blackouts" and "personality shifts."

I wasn't worried.

Not really.

Because I remembered everything.

Or maybe I just remembered the parts loud enough to drown out anything else.

———

The ride home was quiet.

The city rolled by in slow motion, glass and steel and rain-dark pavement. I watched it through the window like a stranger, like I'd never really seen it before.

By the time we pulled into the driveway, my fingers were aching from clenching the door handle.

The house looked the same. Of course it did.

Same sag in the porch railing. Same cracked stone path I always trip on but never fix. Same wind chime Rose insisted wasn't broken even though it only ever rang in one direction.

But it didn't feel right.

None of it did.

My skin prickled, the house an imitation of itself, close enough to pass at a glance, wrong the second you breathed it in.

Inside, the lights were dim and the air too still. The smell of home—coffee grounds, lavender cleaner, something faintly burnt from a candle she forgot to blow out—should've calmed me.

It didn't.

I sat on the couch while she brought me water and fussed with pillows. She kissed my forehead like I was a kid, whispered something soft I didn't catch, and went upstairs to rest.

I stayed in the silence.

The file folder sat on the table.

I should've burned it.

I should've felt relief.

Dante was locked up. DJ had confirmed it. My badge was waiting on a desk somewhere, and for the first time in days, I was back in my own house, surrounded by things I knew.

But it didn't feel like mine anymore.

I walked into the kitchen, opened a cabinet, and stared at a shelf for a solid minute without remembering what I came for.

The longer I stood there, the heavier the silence became. I swallowed hard, suddenly unsure if I'd ever known what I was looking for.

There was no blood here. No sign of what happened.

Because it hadn't happened here.

But that didn't stop my brain from replaying it. Over and over. The look on his face. The way the crime scene techs whispered. The ritual of it all.

I gripped the counter and closed my eyes.

Something was still wrong.

Not with the case. With me.

Like some part of me had been left at that crash site, or maybe pried open when I saw Dante's face and hadn't shut since.

I took a deep breath. It rattled.

"Get it together," I muttered.

But the house was too quiet. The air too still.

And deep down, I knew—

This wasn't over.

Not even close.

CHAPTER
SEVEN

NIKO

The house smelled like cinnamon and toast.

Rose was humming in the kitchen, off-key and carefree, pretending she hadn't just spent the past week living in a hospital chair. I leaned against the doorway, watching her wrestle a jar of peanut butter as if it had personally wronged her.

"Need help?" I asked.

She turned, startled, then smiled. "Only if you've regained full upper body strength."

"I have... just enough to win this fight."

She handed over the jar. I opened it with a satisfying pop and tried not to wince as my ribs protested.

"You okay?" she asked.

"Just a little sore. Nothing new."

She reached out and ran her hand over my cheek. "You look better today."

I smiled. "You're biased."

"I'm married to you, not blind."

I kissed her forehead and sat at the table. She brought over two mugs of coffee and slid one over before sitting across with her toast.

"So," she said, voice casual but a little too light, "do you think you're going to be able to let this go now?"

I frowned, confused.

"Dante," she clarified. "The case. Your dad. All of it."

I leaned back, sipping my coffee. "I think I already have."

The words came out too easily, like reciting a line I'd practiced instead of something I believed. A faint tug pulled at the back of my mind.

She tilted her head. "Really?"

I nodded. "He's behind bars. DJ saw to that. I'm healing. I've got you. What more could I need?"

Her expression softened, but her fingers still toyed with the edge of her sleeve. "You sure?"

"I'm sure," I said gently. "You don't have to worry about me."

She reached across the table and laced her fingers with mine. "Too late. I can't go through this again."

"I know."

We sat like that for a while, warm morning light stretching across the floor, two mugs steaming between us. No ghosts. No monsters.

Just a man who lost his father.

And the woman who almost gave up on him.

Dad's place hadn't changed.

Same olive-green walls. Same crooked picture frame

over the entry table. Same faint smell of aftershave and instant coffee, as if time had paused the second he died.

I closed the door behind me and stood in the silence.

A part of me wanted to turn around and leave before the silence finished swallowing me up. Another part needed to step deeper, to find something I wasn't even sure I wanted to see.

Everything here was him.

The old recliner with the duct-taped armrest. The shelf of crime novels, half dog-eared. The hat rack where he hung the same worn brown fedora he refused to replace.

I should've felt something final.

Instead, I just felt... off.

I moved slowly, touching things without meaning to, the back of the chair, the badge on the shelf, the faded photograph of him standing beside me on my academy graduation day. He looked proud. I looked cocky.

The memory should've comforted me. Instead, it made my stomach twist.

I went to his desk. Papers, pens, an open notepad scrawled with half-thoughts. I didn't look too closely. It felt wrong, like reading a diary I hadn't earned the right to open.

But the longer I stood there, the more I felt that same old itch. The detective in me whispering to open every drawer, flip every page, chase every shadow. And the son in me whispering to leave it all the hell alone.

I sank into his chair and let the quiet wrap around me.

There was no reason for this feeling, no clue, no hidden message, no voice in my head. Just a heaviness.

A weight in my chest that hadn't lifted, even with Dante in custody.

I thought this would bring peace.

But all it brought was static.

A hum in my brain I couldn't shake.

Like there was still a question waiting to be asked.

Or answered.

I sat there a long time, hands folded, eyes on the badge in the frame beside the lamp.

Dad's badge. Retired, polished, revered.

He'd spent his whole life chasing the truth.

And suddenly, I wasn't sure if I'd found mine.

CHAPTER
EIGHT

NIKO

The service was held at a small chapel outside the city, nothing flashy, just brick and wood and a wide window behind the pulpit that let sunlight pour across the casket like God was trying to make it easier to look at.

The front row was full of brass.

Commanders, captains, lieutenants. Full dress uniforms, silver bars catching the light. Rose held my hand the entire time, her thumb tracing small circles on the back of mine.

I didn't say a word.

Didn't move, didn't cry, didn't breathe too deep. I just watched the casket and listened.

One by one, officers stepped up to the podium.

"He was the definition of grit."

"A real son of a bitch on traffic duty."

"But if he had your back, you never had to look over your shoulder again."

They laughed quietly at that, the kind of laughter you

earn after decades of kicking down doors and scraping blood off boots.

Then DJ stood.

He adjusted the mic and cleared his throat. No notes in hand.

"I met Tony Russo my first year in," he said. "I was all nerves and mouth, thought I knew everything because I'd passed a few tests. He saw right through that."

A few heads nodded. They all knew that version of Tony.

"I remember our first call together, a burglary gone sideways in Lower Price Hill. I jumped out of the car so fast, I left the radio behind. Tony didn't yell. He just handed me a spare and said, 'You sprint like that again without backup, I'll let you die tired.'"

Soft chuckles from the crowd.

DJ's voice dropped slightly. "He never said much about his own life. But he always asked about mine. Always made sure I got home. Always remembered if your kid had a game or your sister was in the hospital. He pretended like he didn't care, but he carried every one of us."

He looked at the casket.

"I wouldn't be the man I am without him. And I'll never forget what it meant to ride next to him."

DJ stepped down and sat beside me.

I didn't look at him. Couldn't.

I just stared forward, fingers clenched in my lap, while the service carried on.

And when they finally played taps and folded the flag, when they handed it to me with eyes full of sorrow like it was supposed to help, I nodded.

But inside, I felt nothing but the echo of DJ's words.

He carried every one of us.

And now he was gone.

The service had ended, but no one moved.

The chapel had fallen into that quiet post-funeral hush, soft murmurs, shuffling feet, the sound of tissues crumpling. The kind of silence that asks for something more, even if no one says it.

I sat frozen, flag folded in my lap, pulse drumming behind my ribs.

DJ glanced at me once.

Then Rose leaned in close, her voice barely above a whisper. "You don't have to. But if you want to... now's the time."

I shook my head. My throat was tight.

"Niko," she said, resting her hand over mine. "You don't have to be strong. Not for them. Just for him."

That broke something open.

For a moment, I stayed seated, knuckles white around the folded flag. My legs felt rooted to the floor, like standing might make everything real in a way I wasn't ready for. The room waited—soft, patient, unbearably quiet.

I stood.

Slow. Heavy.

My knees trembled, just enough for me to feel it and hope no one else did. Each breath felt like it had to fight its way out of my chest.

I walked to the podium, the longest walk of my life.

Every step echoed louder, bouncing off stained glass and polished wood. I could feel eyes on me—not judging, just waiting—and that made the air feel even thicker. I kept my gaze fixed on the floor, unsure if looking up would steady me or shatter me entirely.

I didn't look at anyone.

Didn't clear my throat. Didn't check a note.

I just stared out at the room and gripped the edges of the podium, grounding myself, letting the silence settle around me until there was nowhere left to hide.

"My father wasn't easy to love."

That got a few knowing smiles.

"He was loud. Stubborn. Always ten steps ahead of the rest of us and pissed we couldn't keep up. He had opinions about everything, and most of them were wrong. But you'd never convince him of that."

A chuckle rippled through the pews.

"But he showed up. Every time. Every damn time."

I paused. Swallowed hard.

"He wasn't the kind of man who said 'I love you.' Not out loud. But he taught me to tie my first tie before my first funeral. He gave me his backup piece when I made detective. He used to leave gas money in my glove box when he thought I wasn't making enough. He never admitted any of it. Just did it."

My voice cracked. I kept going.

"When I lost a case, he'd buy me a beer and call me soft. When I got promoted, he said it was about time. When Rose and I got married, he danced with her like he'd known her his whole life."

I looked down at the flag in my hands.

"He wasn't perfect. But he was mine. And I would give anything…"

I broke off.

Rose's eyes met mine, glassy and wide.

"I'd give anything to have one more shitty argument

with him about the Bengals or jurisdiction or whether I should eat fewer cheeseburgers."

Laughter again. Warmer this time.

"I miss him," I said simply. "And I'll spend the rest of my life trying to make him proud."

I stepped down before I could fall apart.

DJ was already rising, helping me back to the pew. Rose's hand found mine and squeezed.

And for the first time since the hospital, I let myself cry without apology.

CHAPTER
NINE

NIKO

They were gone.

All of them.

The endless train of badge-polished handshakes and hollow condolences had finally thinned out. The speeches were over. The food trays packed up. The only thing left was a hole in the ground and the man who'd raised me, boxed up inside it.

I stood there long after the last car rolled away. Didn't matter that the sun had dipped or that my legs ached from standing. I couldn't leave. Not yet.

Tony Russo. My father. My partner. My goddamn compass.

Now a nameplate on polished wood.

The wind kicked up, lifting a single leaf and spinning it across the marble headstones like it couldn't decide where to land. I didn't move. Didn't blink. Just stared into the grave as if I could will him to rise and finish this himself.

"I know it was him," I muttered. My voice cracked. "I know it was Dante."

I swallowed, jaw tight. That signature was carved into my brain: the same butchery, the same twisted message. Eyes gone. Tongue removed. Ears sliced clean off.

See no evil. Speak no evil. Hear no evil.

Dante's evil.

I crouched down, fingers brushing the corner of the casket like it mattered. Like he could feel me.

"You always said the law wasn't built for monsters. That sometimes justice came down to the people who gave a damn."

I leaned in, whispering a prayer.

"I give a damn."

The groundskeeper lingered in the distance, not saying a word, just holding the shovel and waiting for the moment to lower him under.

I stood tall. "You've got my word, Dad. I won't let this be the end."

The first shovel of dirt hit the lid like a drumbeat.

I turned my back on it.

Because the man who did this was still out there.

And I wasn't done.

Back home, the quiet hits me harder than the funeral did.

Rose left me with a kiss and a soft promise to give me space. I think she knew it wouldn't help. Grief doesn't need a stage; it performs best in the silence.

I sat on the front steps with the late sun slicing through

the trees, casting long shadows over our tiny patch of yard. My tie was loose. Jacket abandoned. I didn't even notice the crumpled tissue in my fist until DJ pulled up.

He stepped out of his car holding a brown paper bag and a look that said he was trying not to look worried. Typical DJ.

"Got you something." He tossed the bag beside me.

I reached in, expecting whiskey or some cheap diner food. Instead, I pulled out a flask. It was heavy. Worn. The initials *TR* were scratched faintly into the corner.

"Is this—"

"Tony's," he said, sitting down with a grunt. "Gave it to me as a joke when he retired. Told me to use it if you ever turned into a pain in the ass."

I couldn't help the cracked laugh that slipped out. My throat closed around it. "He'd haunt you if you didn't give it to me."

DJ shrugged. "He's going to haunt me anyway. This just buys me some time."

We sat in silence for a while. I gripped the flask because it was the only thing tethering me to solid ground. Then DJ cleared his throat, like he was working up to something worse.

"I, uh... I didn't come alone," he said.

I looked over. "What do you mean?"

"She's waiting in the car. Said she wanted to give you a few minutes to act normal before she ruined it."

"What the hell are you talking about?"

He grunted again, standing with a wince. "Come meet my new partner. Well, temporary partner since you're still technically on light duty. Department's orders."

I groaned. "Jesus, DJ—"

Before I could finish, the passenger side door of his car swung open, and chaos stepped out.

The shift hit me like cold water. My nerves were still raw from the funeral, too exposed for whatever the hell this was. For a second, I felt myself lean back, like her presence came in too fast, too loud.

Combat boots, black jeans, and a T-shirt that said *I Believe in Lizard Rights*. Her purple-dyed hair was twisted into messy space buns with a cigarette behind her ear, and she had at least a dozen enamel pins decorating her leather jacket. One of them said *I see dead people, and they won't shut up*. And a single red string tied around her middle finger like a promise to God or Satan, maybe both.

"Detective Callahan," DJ said, deadpan. "Caz, this is Niko. Try not to get him arrested."

She strode up, pale hazel eyes already scanning me like a crime scene.

It was too much—too direct, too alive. After hours of graveside silence, her intensity felt like someone flinging open all the windows in my skull at once.

"Yo," she said. "Your aura's buzzing like a power line. Love that for you. Hate it for everyone else."

I blinked. "What?"

"She means hi," DJ muttered.

Caz wasn't tall, maybe five-three, but she moved like someone who didn't need to be tall. She stuck out her hand, then pulled it back before I could shake it. "Actually wait, your energy's all grief-drenched and twitchy. Fist bump?"

I hesitated, not sure I could match her energy without

breaking something inside me. My grief still felt like wet cement around my ribs.

I glanced at DJ, who looked like he'd aged ten years in the last two minutes.

He sighed. "This is my life now."

"Not forever," Caz chirped, then looked at me. "Just until you're cleared. Or you snap. Whichever comes first."

I stared at her. "Is she joking?"

DJ rubbed his face. "You'll never know."

And just like that, my quiet grief imploded into whatever the hell this was.

She popped a piece of gum into her mouth as she strutted in like she owned the place.

"So, Niko Russo," she declared, pointing at me like a courtroom witness. "You're taller than I imagined. Like six feet of trauma with a pulse. Your aura's got a weird rattle to it today. Might be the trauma. Or ghosts. I'm the new blood. DJ's babysitter while you're on bedrest."

I raised an eyebrow but shook it off. "I'm not on bedrest."

DJ dropped into the recliner and covered his face. "She's technically effective."

Caz beamed. "That's the nicest thing he's said about me all week."

I exhaled slowly, trying to catch up to the pace she set just by existing. A part of me wanted to tell her to slow down while another part found her chaos a strange, unexpected relief.

"So... what are you doing here?" I asked.

DJ nodded at the flask. "Wanted to make sure you got

that. And figured you should meet her sooner rather than later. She's going to be involved in everything now."

I looked her over. She was already poking through the photos on my fridge like she lived here. Then she turned back and squinted at me.

"You don't believe in gut feelings, do you?" she asked.

"Not really."

"Shame," she muttered, and pulled a notebook out of her jacket. "Because mine are rarely wrong."

DJ looked at me. "She means well. Just... keep the sharp objects out of reach."

Caz snapped her gum. "Only stabbed a suspect once. He was literally asking for it."

I didn't laugh. But I didn't hate her either.

Something about her chaos felt oddly comforting. Like static that kept the real noise out.

Maybe I wasn't ready for peace yet. Maybe static was all I could handle.

CHAPTER
TEN

NIKO

Caz was still orbiting my kitchen like a planet with no gravitational rules, touching everything, smelling some things, and scribbling every so often in a battered notebook held together by duct tape and hope.

She flicked her eyes toward me suddenly. "Okay, orientation time."

DJ groaned behind her. "Caz—"

"No, no, he deserves the full rundown," she said, flipping the notebook open. "Niko needs to know what he's working with."

"I'm not working with you," I said.

"Yet," she corrected, chewing her gum like it owed her money. "Anyway, ground rules: one, don't touch my snacks. Two, don't touch my red string. Three, if I start speaking in third person, just go with it. It's usually a download."

"A what?" I asked.

"Childhood trauma projectiles," she said matter-of-factly. "Anyway, moving on."

She leaned her hip against my counter, arms crossed, expression shifting into something surprisingly human.

"I grew up in foster care," she said. "Bounced around. The weird kid. You know the trope, talks too much, reads too fast, obsessed with serial killers. Wrote letters to them sometimes. Strictly platonic."

I blinked. "You wrote—"

"Shh," she said. "It's character development."

DJ rubbed his forehead like a migraine was forming. "She cracked a cold case at twenty-three by connecting three obscure symbols no one else noticed. That's why they keep her."

"And because I'm fun at parties," she added.

"No one invites you to parties."

"Because they fear my power."

I snorted despite myself.

She turned to me again. "Anyway, I don't do paperwork. I eat exclusively gas station food for 'gut training,' I haven't owned a piece of matching furniture in ten years, and I once got written up for trying to bring a ferret into the station as an emotional support animal."

I didn't even know where to start.

Then she brightened suddenly. "Oh! And I had a dog named Rufus. I loved Rufus. Rufus did not love me. Probably because he was possessed."

DJ shot her a look. "Rufus is dead."

"He lives on," she whispered dramatically. "In the walls."

"Stop telling people that."

"You can't prove it's not true."

Before I could process any of it, Rose walked in with a

plate of cookies because she's incapable of letting anyone leave our house unfed.

"Oh! You must be Caz," she says warmly.

Caz gasped. "Your aura is so green and sparkly. Like a freshly mowed lawn that definitely hides a body underneath it."

Rose blinked. "Thank... you?"

"That's a compliment," DJ said quickly.

"It is," Caz agreed, taking a cookie and sniffing it like she was testing for poison. "I like you. You're married to a detective and you don't have a single conspiracy board in this house. That's... bravery."

Rose shot me a look that basically asked, "Is she serious?"

I just shrugged.

Caz continued, mouth full of cookie. "Anyway, DJ and I just came to bring the flask and make sure you weren't, you know, dead or having visions or seeing shadow people."

"Not yet," I said.

"Rad," she replied.

DJ stood, clapping his hands together. "Alright. We're leaving. Let the man rest."

Caz pointed two fingers at her eyes, then at me. "We'll be in touch, Russo."

She marched out the door like she was leading an army. DJ followed with an exhausted wave.

When the car pulled away, the silence fell hard again.

Rose exhaled. "She's... interesting."

"That's one word for it."

"She seems like she cares."

"She seems like she needs a handler," I muttered.

Rose smirked. "Good thing DJ's used to difficult partners."

I didn't argue. He's dealt with my dad. He's dealt with me.

And despite Caz's chaos, despite the conspiracy jokes and the weird aura commentary...

I didn't hate her. I needed the disruption.

***

Later that night, the house was finally still.

Rose was curled against me, her breath soft against my chest, one leg tucked between mine, trying to hold me in place.

I wasn't going anywhere.

But I also wasn't sleeping either.

My eyes are locked on the ceiling, the shadows above are ghosts I couldn't name.

Every shape looked familiar until it didn't, shifting just enough to make my pulse jump. Grief could do that. So could fear.

The flask sits on the nightstand where I'd left it, untouched. Every time I close my eyes, I hear the dirt hitting wood again.

"You're not asleep," Rose murmured, voice rough with fatigue.

"No," I said quietly.

She shifted, resting her chin on my chest. Her fingers traced slow, aimless lines along my ribcage, sketching a map.

"Is it the funeral?" she asked.

"No... Yes..."

I sighed. "It's everything."

She didn't push. Just waited. That was the thing about Rose—she didn't need every answer right away. She just needed honesty.

"Dante's locked up," I said finally. "The system did its job. There's supposed to be closure in that, right?"

She nodded slowly against me.

"But it doesn't feel like closure," I whispered. "It feels like a loophole. Like something's missing."

Her fingers stopped moving.

The room suddenly felt smaller, like saying the next words might changer something I couldn't undo.

"I need to see him," I said. "Face to face. Not behind glass. Not in court transcripts. I need to look him in the eye and know."

"Niko—" she started.

"I know what you're gonna say."

"Do you?" she asked, propping herself on one elbow. "Because I was going to say you're going to do whatever you set your mind to anyway."

That made me smile. Barely.

She cupped my face, thumb grazing the edge of my jaw. "Niko... I don't know how much longer I can keep supporting you if you're not going to be careful."

"I will."

"No stunts. No lone wolf nonsense."

I kissed her palm. "I'm not alone."

She leaned down and pressed a kiss to my forehead. "Try to sleep tonight. Just a little."

I didn't answer.
Because sleep wasn't coming.
Not until I got answers.
Not until I heard the devil's voice for myself.

CHAPTER
ELEVEN

NIKO

The holding room at Iron Ridge smelled like sweat and rust. Not blood, though somehow that's what I kept tasting.

No bars. No glass. No orange jumpsuit. Just four walls, two chairs, and a man I could kill with my bare hands.

Dante Crowe.

He looked like something that crawled out of a dying fire, all sharp lines and scorched edges. A wiry frame wrapped in state-issued gray, skin pale and stretched tight like it barely fit anymore. His hair was long, dark, and greasy, hanging in uneven clumps that framed a face carved by time and violence. One eye twitched now and then, like a glitch in an old tape. But it was the other eye, the still one, that made my stomach turn. Flat. Cold. Like it had watched people die and never looked away.

His knuckles were raw. Fingernails bitten to the quick. A faint scar curved under his jaw like a smile that didn't belong to him.

My pulse kicked up. Just a little.

I told myself it was the cold. Or the weight of the moment. Or grief.

But something in me, something buried deep, knew better.

I'd seen monsters before. Hell, I'd even arrested some.

But this one?

This one looked like he built them. He sat across from me like this was a meeting. Like we were equals.

He wasn't tall, maybe five-ten, but he felt taller. Like the air stretched to make room for whatever lived behind his eyes.

"Detective Russo," he said. His voice was rough and low, but too casual. "I wondered how long it would take baby boy to show up."

I didn't answer. Not yet.

He watched me with a calm arrogance, like he was the one evaluating me.

"You're quieter than I pictured," he said, leaning forward, elbows on the table. "Your dad had more bark."

"Keep his name out of your fucking mouth."

He smiled. "Touchy."

I let the silence stretch.

"I don't want your games," I said. "I'm not here for a power trip. I'm here because I need to know why."

His smile didn't waver, but his eyes changed. A flicker. A shadow behind the glass.

"Why?" he repeated. "There's no clean answer to that. No perfect headline you can slap on the file."

"Try anyway."

He stared at me, long and hard. Then he leaned back, his chair creaking.

"I was angry," he said. "Angry and broken, and the world kept asking me to behave like I wasn't. I wanted the pain to land somewhere else. So I made it land. Over and over. All it cost were some eyes, ears, and tongues."

He scratched the inside of his wrist. Slow. Methodical.

"I didn't pick your father," he continued. "He picked me. Every time he opened a case. Every time he chased a lead. He couldn't leave the monster under the bed. He had to drag it into the light."

I swallowed. "So you killed him."

"No," Dante said. "I ended him. There's a difference. I killed other people. This one was special."

I stood. The chair screeched across the floor.

Dante didn't flinch. He just looked up at me, head tilted like a dog watching traffic.

"You think locking me up brings balance?" he asked. "That justice is some neat equation?"

I leaned in, close enough to smell the sweat on his skin.

"No," I said. "But looking you in the eye and seeing what a pathetic, hollow bastard you are? That helps."

He grinned again. Not smug. Just entertained.

As I turned to leave, he called after me.

"You'll never stop thinking about me now," he said. "Every noise in the dark, that'll be me. You'll wake up hearing my voice in the quiet. You already do, don't you? Me being locked up doesn't bring anyone back. Especially not your pathetic old man."

I froze in the doorway.

For a split second, my body locked up—not from fear, but from something heavier, colder. A warning, maybe. Or a question I didn't want answered. The words echoed behind me.

I told myself to walk away. To breathe. To be the detective my father raised.

But the room felt smaller with every second I stood there.

Especially not your pathetic old man.

I turned.

Not all at once.

Something inside me whispered *don't*.

But the grief answered louder.

Dante barely had time to blink before I was across the room.

I slammed him into the wall so hard the drywall cracked. My forearm pressed into his throat, pinning him with every ounce of grief I'd tried to swallow since the crime scene.

His feet kicked once.

Then stilled.

"You think this is a game?" I hissed. "You think you get to crawl out of the shadows and gloat?"

His mouth moved. Not words. Just a sick, gurgling grin.

My fingers twitched. Ready to close.

Flashes hit behind my eyes.

My dad's jacket on the hook.

The front door that never opened again.

Rose telling me to let go.

I loosened my grip.

Just enough for him to breathe.

"You're not a phantom," I said. "You're not a nightmare. You're a sad little man who got caught."

He laughed. Quiet. Like it tickled.

"Did I?" he rasped.

I backed off.

Let go.

He slumped against the wall, coughing like he enjoyed the pain. Like it meant he still mattered.

I didn't look back again.

The door clicked behind me as I left.

But the silence that followed?

It wasn't relief.

I don't know what it was.

CHAPTER
TWELVE

NIKO

I don't remember getting back in the car.

One minute I was slamming the door behind me, leaving Dante in that cold gray box like he was someone else's problem, and the next, I was halfway home with the heater blasting and my hands locked tight on the wheel.

My knuckles were white.

My jaw tighter.

I can still feel his throat under my fingers.

Still hear the crack of drywall.

Still see that grin like he wanted to die by my hands. Like it would've made him real again.

The roads blurred past, every streetlight stretching long and liquid across the windshield. I kept checking the rearview mirror, expecting to see him in the backseat.

That eye. That dead-fucking-eye.

I don't know how long I drove. Maybe twenty minutes. Maybe hours. Time bent around the adrenaline.

By the time I pulled into the driveway, my pulse had

slowed, but not by much. I sat there for a minute, engine running, eyes fixed on the porch light.

I wanted a cigarette. I wanted a drink. I wanted to scream.

But mostly?

I wanted to forget that face.

The front door creaked open.

Rose stood in the frame, wrapped in my old hoodie with the sleeves pushed up and her hair tied back. No makeup. Just her. Soft and steady. Beautiful.

Her eyes scanned me like she already knew what I'd done.

"You're late," she said quietly. "You okay?"

She didn't move from the doorway. "Niko… something happened, didn't it?"

Her voice wasn't angry. Just afraid.

I shut off the engine.

Got out without answering.

She didn't press. Just stepped aside to let me in.

The door clicked shut behind me.

And I finally exhaled.

We didn't talk right away.

Rose set a mug of tea on the nightstand and crawled into bed beside me, curling up, trying to lend me her warmth. I lay flat on my back, eyes tracing the cracks in the ceiling that had been there since we moved in.

"God damn it, Niko. I was hoping you wouldn't go see him," she said eventually.

"I had to."

Her voice was intense. "Did it help?"

"Niko," she said, firmer this time, "what did he say to you? Or... what did you do?"

The question hung there, heavy, impossible to dodge.

I let the silence answer.

Her breath caught, just barely. "Jesus..."

Not judgment, just grief, the kind that made my chest cave in even more.

My fingers twitched against the sheets. The ghost of his throat pulsed in my palm. I could smell that sour breath. See that twitching eye.

"He's not human," I said. "He wears the skin, but it's empty underneath. Like he's waiting for someone else to crawl in."

Rose turned toward me, her hand brushing my arm.

"Niko..." She hesitated. "Whatever he is, it's not your burden anymore. He's locked away. You don't have to carry him with you. Please let him go."

"I do," I said. "Because whatever justice looks like, this isn't it. A locked door doesn't balance the scale. It just hides it."

She sighed. "You want to see him again."

I didn't answer.

"Why?" she asked, voice cracking. "What could he possibly give you that you don't already know?"

She wasn't challenging the obsession—she was terrified of where it led.

"You're going to, aren't you?"

I finally looked at her. Her eyes didn't flinch. She wasn't pleading. Just knowing.

"You always do this," she whispered. "You dig until your fingers bleed, and then keep digging."

"I need to understand."

"No," she said. "You need to sleep."

She leaned in and pressed a kiss to my forehead. Her fingers brushed my cheekbone before pulling back.

"I know you're going to do whatever you set your mind to anyway. Just be careful. Don't let him inside. And don't push me away."

I closed my eyes.

But sleep didn't come.

Only the sound of that voice, echoing through the quiet.

You'll never stop thinking about me now.

CHAPTER
THIRTEEN

NIKO

I barely made it out of the shower before the doorbell rang. Rose was already in the kitchen, calling out, "You expecting someone?"

No.

But I had a hunch.

I opened the door wearing damp sweats, hair still dripping, and found DJ standing on the porch with a face like a disappointed dad.

Behind him, grinning like she was about to watch fireworks, was Caz.

"Oh, good," I said, voice flat. "The cavalry."

DJ crossed his arms. "You went to Iron Ridge to see him."

"You checking my calendar now?"

"I'm checking your sanity."

I stepped aside and let them in.

Caz entered and immediately tossed her jacket over the back of the couch like she lived here. "Did you hit him?"

"No," I said.

"Shame."

"Caz," DJ warned.

"What?" she said, grin widening. "I'm just saying, if I knew the guy who gutted my old man was sitting in a room with no glass between us, my fingers would've slipped."

"You're not helping."

"Hey!" she said, dropping into my recliner like it belonged to her. "Don't be rude. I brought gas station muffins."

"You did not."

She smirked. "No, but now you're disappointed and that's way more fun."

DJ ran a hand down his face. "This is serious."

"I know," she said. "But come on, he lived the movie moment. Face-to-face with the monster, pulse pounding, chair scraping across the floor... I'm obsessed."

"I'm concerned," DJ muttered, looking at me.

"Join the club," I said.

He pointed a finger. "You're off the leash, Niko. Light duty doesn't mean vigilante shit. If the captain finds out—"

"I know," I said. "It was one time."

"Famous last words," Caz said, miming air quotes.

DJ turned to her. "Can you not encourage this?"

"Too late. I already made a fan cam in my head."

"Oh my God," he groaned.

Rose peeked into the room, wiping her hands on a dish towel.

"Everything okay in here?"

"Not even a little," DJ said.

"We're bonding," Caz offered.

Rose arched a brow, then gave me a look that said *you better not be bleeding again.*

I shrugged. She disappeared back into the kitchen.

DJ took a long breath, resetting his entire nervous system. "Look, I get it. Closure is messy. But you saw him. It's done. You got what you needed, yeah?"

I glanced at him—really looked at him—for the first time all day.

Did I get what I needed?

The image of Dante's face flashed behind my eyes. That calm, rotting smirk. The way his voice crawled under my skin and stayed there like it belonged.

I thought about what he said: "You'll never stop thinking about me now."

"No," I said quietly. "I don't think I did."

DJ sighed, leaning forward with his elbows on his knees. "Then what are you chasing, man? Because I've seen where the rabbit hole leads, and it's not pretty. You got a wife, a badge, and enough ghosts already. Don't let that piece of shit haunt you on purpose."

Caz, miraculously, said nothing. She just sipped her soda like she was holding a secret.

"I'm not haunted," I said, shaking my head. "But justice… it's not what I thought it'd be. Seeing him behind bars didn't feel like balance. It felt unfinished. Like something's still frayed."

"Then cut the thread before it wraps around your throat."

I raised an eyebrow. "Did you rehearse that one?"

"Little bit," he muttered, cracking a grin.

Caz perked up. "Okay, question. Is this, like, your vibe

now? Brooding, haunted hot cop who stares into the distance a lot? Because if so, we should get you a cape. Or at least a fog machine."

DJ groaned. "Please stop encouraging him. And hot?"

"I'm serious! He could be, like, a tragic detective in a Netflix drama. Just... occasionally stabby."

"Caz."

"What? I'd watch it."

Rose walked in, drying her hands. "Am I interrupting?"

"Nope," I said.

"Yes," DJ said.

"Absolutely," Caz said. "But in a sexy, mysterious way."

Rose blinked. "You good?"

I nodded slowly. "Getting there."

"Want me to kick them out?"

"Yes," DJ said.

"No," I said.

Caz gave Rose a thumbs-up. "I like her."

"She likes you too much," DJ muttered.

Rose tilted her head toward me. "You sure you're okay?"

I met her eyes. The ache was still there, but for the first time since the funeral, it wasn't a scream. Just a hum beneath my ribs.

"I will be."

We all sat there for a while longer, quiet settling over the room in pieces.

And then—Bzzz.

Bzzz.

Bzzz.

Our phones lit up.

Three screens. One message.

Inmate DANTE CROWE unaccounted for.
Status: ESCAPED. Proceed with caution.

The words didn't register at first. They just floated there, unreal, impossible—a glitch in the air.

My stomach bottomed out.

DJ went pale.

His hand hovered over his phone like he wasn't sure the screen would stay the same if he blinked.

Caz whispered, "Holy shit."

The silence after was deafening.

And just like that, the ache became a scream again.

CHAPTER
FOURTEEN

NIKO

The sky was bleeding orange by the time we pulled up to Iron Ridge.

Alarms wailed inside the walls, a sickly mechanical screech that curdled my blood. The gates were wide open, a half-dozen state cruisers scattered like fallen dominoes, lights cutting through the dusk, panic taking shape. Uniforms swarmed the yard, shouting into radios, scanning corners, trying to make order from chaos.

DJ slammed his door before the car even stopped. Caz followed, boots crunching gravel, wired for moments like this.

Me? I just stared.

Dante Crowe was a cold case. A rumor with teeth.

Then we had him.

Now he was smoke.

And we were chasing ghosts again.

Caz nudged me as I stepped out. "You okay?"

I wasn't.

But I nodded anyway.

We moved together, the three of us, slipping through the confusion. No one stopped us—everyone was too busy unraveling.

Inside, the sound shifted. The alarms were louder, harsher.

The air hit colder too—unnaturally cold, like we'd stepped into a freezer instead of a hallway.

Flashing lights strobed across peeling paint and rusted bars. Guards sprinted past, breathless and rattled. One nearly clipped DJ's shoulder but didn't look back.

We reached the security office, a reinforced bunker near the central wing. The steel door hung open. Inside, a wall of monitors flickered, showing every angle of a prison that no longer held what it claimed.

That's when someone noticed us.

But the questions, the explanations... all that would come later.

For now, all I could do was stare at the empty cell on screen.

Even through the grainy footage, the room felt wrong—too still, too sterile, like the air inside it wasn't moving at all. A dead room inside a living building.

Dante's bed was still made, his uniform was neatly folded, and the monster was gone.

"I want every second of footage from the last forty-eight hours," DJ snapped.

The guard at the workstation looked like he wanted to disintegrate. "We're... we're pulling what we can, sir, but there's a gap..."

I stiffened. "What the fuck do you mean, 'gap'?"

The guard glanced at his supervisor, then at the screen.

He dragged the mouse across the timeline. Footage flickered: me choking Dante.

A sharp chill crawled down my spine, the same cold from the hallway tightening around my ribs as the screen stuttered.

Then—

Nothing.

Just static.

Timestamps frozen.

Then—

today.

This morning.

A guard opening the door to an empty cell.

My throat tightened. "You're telling me the surveillance glitched?"

"Only in that room," the guard said. "It was flagged and logged, but no one caught it in time."

Caz let out a delighted cackle. "That's amazing." She clapped once like a kid at a magic trick. "Oh my God, Niko, you actually choked him? You gave him the Vader special. Tell me you left a handprint on his greasy throat."

"Caz," DJ growled.

She grinned wider. "What? It's hot. Vigilante daddy laying down the law. Didn't know we had a Xaden Riorson shadow daddy in the squad."

DJ pinched the bridge of his nose. "You're not helping."

"So you keep saying," she sang.

I didn't react. Couldn't.

My jaw was tight. My fists tighter. My heartbeat hammered against my ribs.

"Is this real?" I asked quietly, staring at the cut in the footage.

The head of security stepped forward, sweat pooling at his collar. "We believe the tampering was internal. Someone on the tech team may have been compromised. We aren't ruling anything out. But Crowe is gone. And this footage is the last known visual."

DJ muttered something under his breath. Probably a prayer.

Caz leaned closer to the monitor. "Well, I'll be damned. You did look hot doing it."

DJ threw her a look that could kill. "Enough. We'll talk about this later."

She backed off, barely suppressing another giggle.

But none of it touched me.

Because staring at that static screen—

Watching that phantom cut in the timeline—

I knew exactly what it meant.

Dante Crowe didn't escape.

He vanished.

And whatever helped him...

Wasn't finished yet.

CHAPTER
FIFTEEN

NIKO

The bullpen was louder than usual. Phones rang, printers whirred, someone cursed about the coffee being out—background chaos that had always felt familiar. But today, it felt like static. Just noise I couldn't quite tune into.

Stepping through the felt doors felt like stepping into a new life. Maybe I was.

A few heads turned. Some nodded. Others looked away.

Nobody said it, but they all knew. I'd visited Dante Crowe the day before he escaped. The timing alone was enough to put a target on my back.

DJ met me at the entrance to the main floor. His jaw was tight, arms crossed.

"You're cleared," he said. "Brass fast-tracked it. Technically, you never stopped being active duty. They just needed to cover their ass until things settled."

I raised a brow. "So they settled?"

"Not even close," he muttered. "But the higher-ups need

a scapegoat or a savior. Guess which one they want you to be."

He handed me a file. My name was on the front.

"I thought this was a cold case again," I said, flipping it open.

"Not anymore." DJ glanced toward the bullpen. "You're lead. They want Dante back in a cage. And they want it clean."

DJ hesitated, just long enough for me to catch it, worry flickering across his face. His fingers lingered on the file, clearly unsure if he should be handing it to me at all.

I snapped the folder shut and exhaled through my nose.

"Welcome back, Detective," came a familiar voice behind me.

Caz. Leaning on the doorway, oversized sunglasses indoors, coffee in one hand, smugness in the other.

"You hear they're keeping me on the case even though you're back?" she said, grinning. "Apparently my charm's too much for Internal Affairs to handle."

"She threatened to fake a hostage situation if they didn't keep her on," DJ muttered. "Swear to God."

Caz raised her cup in a toast. "Sometimes the only way out is through, babe."

I smirked despite myself. The ache behind my eyes hadn't gone away since last night. I hadn't told Rose every-thing—not yet—but the weight of it pressed heavy on my chest.

I was back. But I wasn't whole.

"You look like hell," Caz said, falling in beside me as we walked toward our desks.

"Thanks," I said.

"Sexy hell, though."

DJ groaned. "Can we not flirt in the middle of a manhunt? And he's fucking married."

Caz gave him finger guns. "Don't be jealous. You're still my work husband. Well, actually you're kinda like my work dad, so scratch that."

He turned to me. "We're all officially on the Crowe case now. You, me, her. Congrats. The dream team. Or the therapy group. Take your pick."

DJ's eyes met mine for a second. Not the usual partner look, but something tighter, like he was bracing for the fallout of letting me lead again.

I looked down at the folder again. Dante's name stared back at me. It never left.

"Let's bring the motherfucker home," I said.

Caz tilted her head. "Alive, right?"

I didn't answer.

About an hour later, DJ cornered me near the briefing room. No folder this time—just his phone in one hand, jaw clenched tighter than usual.

"Got a weird one," he said. "You ever heard the name Toby Huntley?"

I shook my head. "Should I have?"

"Maybe not. He wasn't on any of the original Crowe files. Never popped in our databases. But he just called dispatch. Real quiet. Real shaky."

"Anonymous?"

"Not quite. He gave a first name, dropped a few breadcrumbs. Sounded like he was hiding in a bathroom, whispering like someone was about to kick in the door."

My pulse ticked up. "What'd he say?"

"Said he saw Dante. In person. Recently."

I blinked. "He saw him and called it in?"

"That's the weird part. He didn't call to help—he called because he's scared shitless. Didn't give an address. Didn't even confirm what city he's in. Just said, and I quote, 'I saw him. He's out. You have no idea what he's planning. If he knows I talked, I'm dead.' Then he hung up."

"Jesus," I muttered.

DJ nodded grimly. "We traced the signal. Burner phone bouncing off a couple towers near Westwood and Clifton. Could've been anywhere in that radius. Hell, could've been moving."

"So he's terrified, maybe running, maybe hiding—and the only thing he did was call us to almost help."

"Exactly. I don't think he trusts cops. And I don't think he's going to trust anyone unless we find a way to reach him directly."

"What else do we know about him?"

"Almost nothing. But I ran a few fast checks. There's a Toby Huntley who used to bartend in Lower Price Hill. No record. No priors. Used to crash with some of Crowe's old circles back in the day but dropped off the map when the murders started."

I rubbed my jaw. "You think he saw something back then?"

"Could be. Could also be that Dante didn't kill him for a reason. Maybe he was useful. Or maybe Toby knew how to stay invisible."

"If he really saw Dante..." I trailed off. The implications crawled under my skin. "We need him. Before Crowe gets to him first."

"Yeah," DJ said. "We need to figure out how to earn his trust and bring him in. Carefully. He sounds like the type who'll bolt the second he hears sirens."

I stared past the window, the city humming outside, not knowing what kind of monster had slipped through its cracks.

"Let's find Toby," I said. "Whatever it takes."

CHAPTER
SIXTEEN

NIKO

The TV flickered across the living room, but neither of us was watching. Rose sat curled at the end of the couch, feet tucked beneath her, wearing the same oversized hoodie she'd stolen from me months ago. I stood behind the armchair, heart pacing to a different rhythm than the laugh track.

"I got reinstated," I said.

She looked over, remote still in her hand. "What?"

"Back on active duty. As of this morning."

She paused, then clicked the TV off.

"So that's it?" she asked. "You're just back in it like nothing ever happened?"

"No. Not like nothing happened. But they need me. Crowe is out—"

"And?" Her voice sharpened. "They have plenty of detectives. Why you?"

"Because I know him," I said. "Because he knows me. Because I can stop this before anyone else gets hurt."

She stood, arms crossed now. "Or before you get hurt. Again."

I didn't answer.

"You don't sleep," she said. "You barely eat. You zone out in the shower like you're chasing ghosts. And now you want to throw yourself right back into the thing that broke you."

"It didn't break me," I muttered.

"Didn't it?"

I looked at her. Really looked. The lines around her eyes. The quiet ache in her mouth. The fear she couldn't hide.

"You think this is an obsession," I said.

"I know it is." Her voice cracked, soft and furious. "And I think if you keep going like this, it's not gonna end with Crowe behind bars. It's gonna end with you in the ground. Or behind bars yourself. And I can't—I won't watch that happen."

I stepped forward. "Rose—"

"No. Listen to me, Niko." She dropped her arms. Her voice went low. "I love you. But you're starting to love the chase more than your own life. More than our life."

Her words hit something raw. Not sharp like a blade—dull like a bruise that never healed.

"You knew what I was when you married me," I said.

"I knew you were a good man trying to make the world better," she whispered. "Now I don't know if you're trying to save people or punish yourself."

We stood there, silent, the space between us thick enough to drown in.

She turned away first and headed for the bedroom.

"I'll sleep on the couch," I said.

She didn't answer. Just closed the door.

And for the second time that day, I felt like I was chasing something I could never catch.

———

I couldn't sleep.

The couch groaned under my weight as I shifted for the third time in ten minutes. The throw blanket Rose left folded never quite covered everything—my feet stuck out, cold and restless. I stared at the ceiling hoping it had answers. Hoping it might crack open and offer something useful.

The room was quiet, but not peaceful. Too quiet. The kind of silence that hums under the skin. The kind that carries thoughts like disease.

I replayed the conversation again. The way she looked at me—tired, scared, almost resentful. Like every step I took toward Crowe pulled me further from her.

Was she wrong?

I rubbed my face, breath shallow. The fridge clicked behind the kitchen wall. A pipe groaned in the ceiling.

But it wasn't the house keeping me awake.

It was him.

Dante's voice scraped under my skin. That sick grin. The way he tilted his head like he was listening to my soul rot.

You'll never stop thinking about me now.

I sat up, chest tight. Tried to tell myself I was just over-whelmed. Just wired. But it felt deeper. His shadow was stitched to mine now, following me through every waking second. Part of me had always been waiting to meet him—and now that I had, I couldn't unsee it.

I checked the time. 1:46 AM.

Fuck.

I got up and moved to the kitchen. The floor was cold under my heels. I poured a glass of water but didn't drink it. Just stared into the sink like something might crawl out.

I couldn't keep doing this.

But I didn't know how to stop.

The bedroom door opened quietly. Rose stood there in the dark, arms crossed, hoodie sleeves too long for her hands.

"You okay?" she asked.

I nodded. Lied.

She didn't push.

Instead, she crossed the room and wrapped her arms around my waist. Rested her head on my chest. I didn't realize how badly I needed it until she was there. Real. Warm. Still mine—for now.

"You're not alone," she whispered.

I wanted to believe her.

But in the back of my mind, something else whispered louder.

He's still out there.

And he's waiting.

CHAPTER
SEVENTEEN

NIKO

We were back at Iron Ridge before the sun had burned off the morning haze. The alarms were off now, but the air still buzzed like the walls remembered them.

Dante's cell sat at the end of the corridor—quiet, untouched, wrong. Even from the doorway I could tell something had shifted. Or maybe it was just me. Maybe standing here again made the floor tilt.

DJ stepped inside first. "We tore this place apart last night," he said. "Maintenance checked vents, plumbing, wiring. No weak points. No tunnels. No blind spots. Nothing."

"Except the video glitch," I muttered.

"Except that," he agreed.

Caz strode in after us, hands on her hips, sunglasses on even though we were indoors. She kicked the metal bed frame like she expected it to hit back.

"Okay, I'm just gonna say it," she announced. "You're all

thinking escape plan and inside job, but clearly the man turned into a bat."

DJ didn't even look up. "Caz."

"A very angry bat," she continued, examining the ceiling like she expected claw marks. "Probably hissed at the guards and then poof, right out the vents."

"Caz," DJ repeated, slower.

I rubbed the back of my neck. "He didn't turn into a bat."

"You don't know that," she argued. "Have you ever actually seen him in daylight? Boom. Checkmate."

I shook my head. DJ sighed so hard something in him evaporated.

Caz crouched by the toilet, poking around with a pen. "Listen, I'm not saying he's a vampire, but if he popped up and started monologuing about immortality, I'd be like yeah, that tracks."

DJ pinched the bridge of his nose. "Please stop."

"Never."

I stepped deeper into the room, tuning her out. The cell was too neat. Too staged. The folded clothes. The made bed. Even the floor looked swept.

Dante wasn't neat. He was methodical. Ritualistic. But neat? No.

This felt like someone playing dress-up with a ghost.

I walked to the back wall and traced the cold concrete. "This isn't right," I said. "He didn't plan this alone."

DJ looked over. "You think someone inside helped him?"

"I think someone on the outside did."

Caz perked up. "You mean like a girlfriend? Or a cult? Or a vampire coven?"

"For the love of—Caz," DJ snapped.

"What? I'm brainstorming."

I crouched near the bedframe. Something bothered me. The air felt wrong. Like the room had been emptied by something more deliberate than a prison search.

"We need to talk to Huntley," I said finally. "He saw something. Otherwise he wouldn't have called."

DJ nodded. "Assuming he hasn't run off again."

Caz spun a pen between her fingers. "Assuming Dante didn't fly into his window and drain his soul."

We both stared at her.

"No bat jokes," DJ said.

"Fine," she muttered. "But when he sprouts wings, don't come crying to me."

I ignored her and stood.

"Let's go," I said. "We're wasting time. Huntley's scared, and scared people run. If we don't find him first, Dante will."

Caz pointed at me with her pen. "So basically, we beat the vampire to the snack. Got it."

DJ groaned again.

But me?

I couldn't shake the feeling that the room wasn't just empty.

It was waiting.

———

We found nothing.

I don't know what I was expecting. Maybe a clue. Maybe an answer.

We got neither. No idea how Dante escaped. No new lead on Toby.

Nothing.

Rose wasn't happy when I got home. The fight wasn't going away.

She was already in the kitchen when I stepped inside—barefoot, arms crossed, back against the sink, trying to hold up the whole house by herself. Her hair was damp from a shower. No makeup. Just her. Raw. Real. Furious.

"You didn't answer my texts," she said.

I dropped my keys in the bowl. "Didn't see them."

"Bullshit."

I didn't argue. Not because she was wrong, though she was right, but because I didn't have the strength.

She followed me into the living room like a shadow with sharp edges.

"You went to the prison," she said. "After everything. After yesterday. You went back there."

I sank onto the couch, rubbing my temples. "I had to."

"No, Niko. You chose to. That's different."

The silence was heavy. Her breathing wasn't.

"I'm not doing this with you right now," I muttered.

"You don't get to not do this. You're spiraling again, and I'm not going to stand by and watch you burn down what's left of our lives just so you can chase a ghost."

"He's not a ghost," I said. "He's out there."

"And you think you're the only one who can stop him?"

I looked up at her.

Her eyes were wet.

Shit.

"I'm your wife," she said. "But I'm starting to feel like collateral damage. Every time you get close to this case, I lose more of you."

"You don't understand what it's like—"

"No," she snapped. "I don't. Because I didn't grow up with a badge and a gun and a father who bled in the street. I just married the man who did. And now I'm stuck watching him self-destruct."

I stood. Too fast.

She flinched.

Something in my chest cracked at the sight of it... Not pain or anger, just a cold certainty that I was losing her one inch at a time.

Not because she was afraid of me.

Because she was afraid for me.

"I'm still me," I said, voice low.

"Are you?"

The worst part was that for a split second, I didn't know how to answer.

But she didn't wait for an answer anyway. She turned and walked down the hall, the bedroom door clicking shut behind her like a verdict.

Guess I was on the couch again.

CHAPTER
EIGHTEEN

NIKO

The station was quieter than usual. Not calm—just tired. Everyone was working the Dante case in some capacity, but nobody was getting anywhere. It felt like chasing smoke through a mirror maze.

I sat in the briefing room, half-listening to DJ argue with Caz about jurisdictional nonsense when my phone buzzed. Unknown number.

Voicemail.

I stared too long before DJ noticed.

"Something?" he asked.

I played the message on speaker:

Hi, this is... this is Toby Huntley. I called before but I don't want trouble, okay? I just... I saw someone. I think it was the guy from the news. Dante Crowe. But I'm not going to tell you where. I can't. I have a kid. I've seen what happens to people who talk. I just... I don't know what to do. Please don't trace this. Just—just leave me alone. But I had to tell someone.

The room went still.

DJ cursed under his breath.

"That's our Toby," Caz said, eyes wide. "Has to be."

"He's scared," I said. "Won't come forward. But that means he knows something."

"He's probably off-grid," DJ muttered. "Somewhere quiet. Remote."

Caz crossed her arms. "So what do we do? Knock on every trailer park and convenience store between here and nowhere?"

"No," I said. "We make him feel safe. Reach out without spooking him. Let him know we aren't the threat."

DJ arched a brow. "And how do you propose we do that, Dr. Phil?"

"I'll record a message. From me. Direct. Honest."

"You think he'll hear your voice and come running?"

"No. But maybe he'll come talking."

I stepped into the hallway, holding my phone like a confession booth.

I hit record.

"Toby. My name is Niko Russo. I'm the lead detective on this case—and the son of the man Dante Crowe murdered. I'm not calling as a cop right now. I'm calling as someone who knows what it means to be afraid. You don't have to tell me where you are. Not yet. Just... let me hear your voice again. If you saw him—if you know something—we'll protect you. We'll keep your kid safe. I swear to you. You're not alone in this."

I sent it. Stared at the screen like the reply would be instant.

DJ leaned in from the doorway. "You sure you're not too close to this?"

"Too late to ask that now."

Caz wandered up beside him, arms crossed. "Should've sent a shirtless selfie with it. Scared or not, that man would swoon."

"Jesus, Caz," DJ groaned.

"What? He clearly has a thing for trauma. Might as well use it."

I rolled my eyes and slid my phone back into my pocket. It buzzed immediately.

Voicemail.

I played it on speaker:

Hey, um... it's Toby. Detective Russo. I—I believe you. I really do. I just... I don't know what to do. He was in the woods. About a mile off the highway near Exit 34. I live nearby, I heard something and... and I saw him. But I'm not crazy, okay? It could've been him. I'll send the location. Just... please hurry. I don't know if he saw me. I don't feel safe.

There was silence. Then a second, shorter message came through.

"Forget it. I said too much. I'm getting out of here. Don't come looking for me."

But the pin was already sent. A map link. Deep woods, off the highway. Remote. Isolated.

DJ looked at me. "We go now?"

I nodded. "We go now."

The sun was low by the time we reached the location—trees draped in gold, shadows stretching like claws across the dirt.

DJ slowed the cruiser. "This is it."

Caz frowned. "It's giving Deliverance, but make it murder-vibe chic."

We parked off the shoulder of an old service road. According to the pin, Toby had seen Dante somewhere past the ridge.

We hiked.

Branches clawed at my jacket. Leaves snapped underfoot. The deeper we went, the quieter the world became. No cars. No birds. Just breath.

"Supposed to be near that bend," DJ said.

We found nothing.

No struggle. No camp. No tracks. Nothing that suggested Toby had ever been there.

"Maybe he panicked," I said. "Maybe he left before Dante could find him."

Caz tilted her head. "Or maybe Dante didn't find him here. Maybe we're too late."

I scanned the woods again, jaw tight.

"Alright," DJ said. "Spread out. Ten minutes."

We did.

And we found nothing.

No blood. No scent. No sound.

Just cold earth and an ache that crept into my spine.

We regrouped. DJ looked frustrated. Caz looked wired. I felt hollow.

Something had happened out here. I could feel it in my bones.

But nothing remained.
Not yet.
We'd try again tomorrow.

CHAPTER
NINETEEN

NIKO

The same road looked different in daylight.

No longer haunting—just empty.

We parked near the tree line. Fog clung to the ground like breath on glass.

"Keep your eyes open," DJ muttered. He sounded tired. We all did.

Caz cracked her neck. "If he's alive, he better have coffee and a fucking apology."

We moved in, retracing yesterday's steps.

This time, we didn't have to go far.

DJ stopped first, arm shooting out to block me. "Shit— don't look."

I looked anyway.

Toby Huntley sat slumped against the base of a tree, blood soaking his shirt, chest caved in. His eyes were gone. Ears too. Tongue gone.

Same M.O.

Same signature.

He was here.

Caz stepped back, hand over her mouth. "He didn't even stand a chance. Dante is killing again."

DJ crouched. "Body's still warm."

Which meant—

No. No no no—

"Jesus Christ," I whispered, backing up.

DJ looked up at me. "You okay?"

I nodded too quickly.

But my heart was doing something ugly. Loud. Off-beat.

DJ stared at me.

"What?"

I shook my head. "Nothing. I'm tired. Didn't sleep."

Caz paced, muttering about tracks and prints, but all I could do was stare at Toby's ruined face.

He was trying to help.

And now he was another victim in a growing line of bodies. Another tally in a blood-stained string that was beginning to circle me tighter and tighter.

I couldn't breathe.

I needed air.

I needed—

Out.

The smell followed us back to the precinct—iron and rot, clinging to our clothes like smoke.

DJ tossed the preliminary report onto the table. Caz didn't sit. She hovered by the whiteboard, arms crossed, foot tapping.

I stared at nothing until DJ finally broke the silence.

"It's him," he said. "Same mutilation pattern. Same organ removal. Tongue, ears, eyes—all gone."

I nodded. I'd known the second he told me not to look.

"There was more blood this time," DJ continued. "Chest wasn't just punctured. It was... pulverized."

Caz chimed in, a little too eager. "You think he was angry? Or in a rush?"

DJ shrugged. "Could be either. Could be both."

I forced my hands still. They kept twitching in my lap. Muscle memory. Ghost pain.

"He's escalating," I said. "Toby wasn't just a message. He was a warning."

Caz looked over, eyes sharp. "Yeah. And we missed it."

DJ sighed. "We didn't have a location until it was too late."

"We have one now," I said. "And we tear it apart."

They both nodded. No argument. Just the hum of the hunt coming alive again.

And somewhere deep inside me, something stirred.

It felt like anticipation.

CHAPTER
TWENTY
DANTE

He walked like he mattered, like the pavement belonged to him, like the cracks and oil stains and broken glass had never cut him before. He kept checking his phone, his reflection, the time, never once checking behind him. They rarely do. That's how I know who's meant to die. The ones who never look back.

Oh, Toby. He was already fading before I touched him. Just another blur of a man, smudged at the edges, drifting too far from the center of the world to matter to anyone but me.

He turned toward the woods, and something in me sighed. Like a switch flipping. Like a song starting. Like I'd done this before, not just once, but over and over in lives I couldn't quite remember, with hands that always ended up soaked and shaking but never regretting. Not really.

The air back there smelled like rot and burnt meat. The kind of stench that clings to your skin. I followed him anyway.

He must've heard me. Maybe not with his ears, but with that ancient part of him, the part people spend their whole lives trying to ignore. The part that whispers: You're not alone. The part that only wakes up right before you die.

He turned. And for one moment, one frozen, perfect breath, he looked right at me. Eyes wide. Lips parted. Heart begging.

He recognized me.

Not who I was. But what I was.

He started to say something, a question or a plea, but I didn't give him the time. I stepped into the space between us like it belonged to me, and everything else faded. The trees. The air. The heartbeat. It all went quiet. It always does.

I think I smiled. I think I whispered something soft and final, but I never remember that part. It always goes missing.

Because after that, it's only blood.

And silence.

And the warmth that comes after.

Like slipping into the skin of something I was always meant to be.

He didn't fall all at once. They never do. It's more like a surrender, a slow melting of the legs, the spine folding in on itself as if the body suddenly remembers gravity was always stronger than hope. I caught him before he hit the ground, not out of mercy, but out of necessity. The work is cleaner when they're held.

He trembled against me, those little useless spasms of a terrified brain firing off its last instructions. His breath hitched, short and sharp, fogging against my collar as if he was trying to leave a part of himself behind.

I lowered him gently.

The violence never starts with a rush.

It starts with a ritual.

I pressed my thumb into the soft skin beneath his eye, just enough pressure to feel the delicate shape of the socket, the thin bone separating the living from the inevitable. He whimpered, a pathetic little sound that fluttered out of him like a dying moth.

"Shh," I whispered, though I don't know why. Maybe habit. Maybe kindness isn't always separate from cruelty.

Then I pushed.

The eye came free easier than people imagine. There's resistance, a wet meaty resistance, but once the membrane gives, it slides warm and slick into my hand. He screamed, or tried to, but it broke halfway out of his throat, turning into fractured noise that barely sounded human.

See no evil.

His other eye took longer. I don't know if he fought harder or if I simply enjoyed the struggle more, but the sound he made when it finally tore loose was almost musical. A sharp, choked wail that bled into a gurgle.

His hands clawed at the ground. At me. At nothing.

I wasn't done.

Hear no evil.

The ears are trickier. Too much cartilage, too much shape. You have to slice through the curve at the right angle or it drags. I used my thumb and forefinger to pull one taut, then tore downward. The skin split like old fabric. His body jerked so violently I had to pin his shoulder with my knee.

The second ear was easier. Practice makes perfect.

Speak no evil.

The tongue is always last. Always. There's a moment when they recognize what's coming, and even blind and half-deaf they know. That dread rolling off them is intoxicating. He tried to clamp his jaw shut. I broke it with the heel of my palm. The crack echoed through the alley like a distant gunshot.

I reached into his mouth.

Warm. Slick. Alive.

I pulled it free, and the sound he made then wasn't a scream. It was a wet, guttural sob that didn't know what shape to take.

His blood coated my wrists, my forearms, dripping to the pavement in thin red strings.

When it was over, he slumped back, body twitching with the last confused signals of a dying nervous system. I watched him go, not with malice or thrill, but with the calm certainty of someone checking off a necessary task.

And when his chest finally stilled, I stood up and breathed in the quiet.

There's a peace in this part.

A stillness nothing else gives me.

For a moment, nothing exists but the pulse fading from my ears and the metallic warmth on my tongue.

Then I walk away, as I always do, stepping over the blood that spreads toward my feet like it wants to follow.

It never does.

CHAPTER
TWENTY-ONE

NIKO

Second victim.

No pattern. No connection. Just like Toby.

Just like my father.

This time it's a woman. Late forties. Lived alone. Paralegal for a downtown firm. Took her lunch late and didn't come back.

They found her in a parking garage stairwell, tucked into the shadows like she had just lain down to rest.

Only she didn't rest.

Same loss of eyes, ears, and tongue. Same calm, surgical brutality.

DJ's the one who tells me. Voice low. He looks like he hasn't slept either.

"Same as the others," he mutters. "There was a camera near the elevator, but it's glitchy. Guess which floor didn't save."

Caz is pacing already. "He's taunting us. This isn't random. He's getting off on the misdirection."

"I thought Toby was a one-off," DJ says. "Some panic kill. But this is back to controlled. He's not spiraling. He's planning."

We're standing in the bullpen like it's a crime scene itself.

Quiet voices. Jittery hands. Nobody says what we're all thinking.

Dante's escalating. Fast.

I haven't said a word since the update came in. I'm staring at the evidence board, and it's staring back.

Toby's photo is up there. Now there's a new one beneath it.

Two dead in less than a week.

We have to check it out.

When we arrive, they brief us quick and clinical, but nothing prepares me for what the officers found in her hands.

He was here.

A photograph.

Wrinkled. Old. Ink fading at the edges.

Two sons.

Both grown.

Both smiling like they hadn't known a hard day in their lives.

It was placed carefully in her lap.

Deliberately.

Not dropped.

Not fallen.

Not incidental.

And the blood—

there's a streak across one of the boys' cheeks, a thin diagonal smear like someone brushed their thumb over it.

It's faint. Easy to miss.

But once you see it, you can't unsee it.

Caz notices it too.

She leans in, squinting.

"Is that... staged?" she murmurs.

No one answers her.

But we all know the truth.

This wasn't panic.

This wasn't rushed.

This was careful.

Intentional.

A message shaped in silence and blood.

I stare at the photo longer than I should. Something tightens inside me. Not recognition. Not memory. More like a pull, like I'm supposed to understand what this means. Like the killer left it for me.

I shake it off.

Focus.

Facts.

Evidence.

Procedure.

But as DJ talks, as Caz paces, as the precinct buzzes around us—

I keep thinking about that photo.

Why she had it.

Why he chose it.

Why he placed it in her hands like it meant something.

A message doesn't need words to be understood.

And somehow, this one feels like it's meant for me.

DJ brought in one of Dante's old colleagues for questioning. Calvin Ross didn't look like a killer. He looked like a man who hadn't slept, shaved, or spoken to another person in days.

I sat across from him in Interview Room 2, watching him chew the inside of his cheek raw.

"You were close with Dante," I said.

He shook his head. "Was. Long time ago. We got drunk a few times. He was funny back then. Kind of a dick, but he was my dickhead, you know?"

DJ stood in the corner, arms crossed. Silent backup.

I pressed. "When's the last time you saw him?"

Calvin's eyes darted. "Couple months before the... that thing with your dad."

I flinched. He saw it.

"Look, I didn't know he was gonna do that," Calvin said. "He ghosted me after. Wouldn't pick up. Changed his number. I figured he left town."

I leaned in. "And yet here we are, bodies showing up with his signature."

Calvin scoffed. "You think I'm helping him? You think I'm with him?"

I said nothing. Just let the silence hang.

He cracked first. "I haven't seen him. I haven't heard from him. If he's out there, he doesn't want me knowing about it."

DJ and I stepped out of the room thirty minutes later,

completely empty-handed.

Another dead end.

I wasn't even supposed to stop.

Just needed a drink. Something with caffeine and sugar and the promise of a few more hours awake without spiraling.

The gas station lights flickered in that headache rhythm that makes you feel like your pulse is broken. Neon buzzed over cracked asphalt and smeared glass.

I pushed the door open. Got hit with the usual cocktail of burnt coffee, synthetic air freshener, and freezer frost.

The girl at the counter looked up.

She couldn't have been more than twenty-two. Too young to be looking at me with that kind of fear. Too young to already understand the shape of monsters.

Petite frame, like anxiety had whittled her down. Black bob, razor-chopped uneven and probably self-cut. Her bangs were too short and a little crooked—it made her look endearing, not sloppy.

She had a pierced nose and dark brown eyes that flicked from me to the shelves to the front door and back again, like she was wired for danger.

Her hoodie swallowed her. Sleeves frayed at the cuffs. My Chemical Romance logo half-faded across the chest. Loose denim cuffed at the ankle. Frayed canvas backpack slouched behind the register like a well-traveled pet.

"Rough night?" she asked, voice a touch scratchy as if

she hadn't spoken to another human in hours. She clocked the badge on my belt.

I grabbed a soda and a pack of gum. "Yeah."

"You're a cop, right?"

"Mmhm. Detective."

"Let me guess. Chasing that guy who broke out? The one who killed all those people?"

My spine tensed. "Something like that."

She hesitated, then leaned in a little, lowering her voice. "I think I saw him."

That got my full attention.

"What?"

"I mean maybe. A guy that looked a lot like him. Came in here a couple nights ago. Same face. Real intense stare. Didn't buy anything. Just... looked at me."

My heart thumped harder. "Did you get a name? A license plate?"

"No. He was on foot." She tapped the counter with nervous fingers, bitten nails chipped with black polish. "But it wasn't just once. I think I've seen him two, maybe three times now. Always late. Always quiet. Just... watching."

Christ. She was practically a kid working alone in a fluorescent box while a predator circled.

"Why the hell didn't you call someone?"

She winced. "I don't know. Thought I was losing it. Thought if I said it out loud it'd become real."

"It's already real."

Her eyes locked onto mine, dead serious now. "You're scared."

I didn't respond. Just reached for my card.

"Maya Sloan," she said before I could ask. "I work nights here. Most nights."

"You see him again, you call me. Immediately. Don't try to be brave. Don't talk to him. Don't even look at him."

She nodded fast, then covered a nervous laugh with the back of her hand.

"I'm not brave. I'm barely holding my shit together most nights."

"Join the club," I muttered.

I walked out with my soda and the creeping suspicion I had just spoken to a ghost before it realized it was one.

CHAPTER
TWENTY-TWO

DANTE

She was already running. That made it more fun.

The soft slap of her sneakers echoed up the concrete stairwell like the panicked pulse of a trapped animal. I followed two flights behind. I didn't rush. I didn't need to. She was making too much noise to think straight, every footfall, every sob, every frantic gasp a breadcrumb leading me right to her.

I could smell her fear in the air. That metallic sweat. That heat behind her panic.

She slammed through the door onto the third floor, fumbling for her keys. The fluorescent bulbs overhead buzzed like dying flies, casting everything in a flickering, jaundiced haze. Her car was close, four or five spaces away. She knew it. She could see it. She just couldn't make her hands work.

I let the stairwell door creak shut behind me.

She spun. Eyes wide. Mouth trembling.

She almost screamed.

Almost.

The blade went in under her chin and up through the soft flesh of the roof of her mouth. Her scream strangled into a wet gurgle, blood erupting from her lips like a broken faucet. She dropped instantly, knees cracking against concrete, but I caught her before her head hit the ground. She didn't get to die that easy.

For a moment, the way her weight sagged into me reminded me of holding someone tired, someone trusting.

We both went down together.

Her in horror.

Me in euphoria.

I straddled her chest and watched the life tear its way out of her throat. Her legs kicked uselessly against the parking lines. Her hands clawed weakly at my jacket, then at the air, then at nothing. A high, rattling wheeze came from her as blood soaked the front of her hoodie and pooled beneath her curls.

She was trying to say something.

Maybe my name.

Maybe God's.

But there's only one name that matters anymore.

And it's mine.

Her eyes bulged. Her jaw slackened. I leaned close to her cheek and listened to the last flutter of her breath like it was a bedtime story. Warm. Sticky. So quiet.

And then she stopped.

Just like that.

Still. Beautiful. Mine.

I sat with her for a long time, the neon hum above us painting her body in ghost-light. I ran my fingers through the blood leaking from her ears. Studied the way it shimmered on the tile. Rubbed a bit of it between my fingers.

I think she had music playing in her car. A sad song.

Perfect.

After I removed her eyes, ears, and tongue, the world finally went quiet enough for me to think.

I always liked the quiet. Even as a kid. Silence felt like someone finally remembering not to yell.

People don't realize how loud a body is, even after death. The twitching. The settling. The tiny air pockets escaping. The subtle complaints of flesh realizing it doesn't need to hold itself together anymore.

But once I took the pieces that mattered, the parts that define how a person receives the world, she went still in a way that felt almost grateful.

The stairwell smelled like copper and dust. The perfect cathedral.

I worked slowly.

Steady hands.

Even breaths.

No rush.

This part mattered more than the killing ever did.

I propped her upright against the concrete wall, her head slumped just enough to suggest she was still trying to look at me. Blood dripped in thin, lazy trails from the hollow sockets, tracing quiet rivers down her cheeks before the warmth cooled and the red turned tacky.

She looked peaceful without her tongue. Cleaner. As if silence had always been her natural state.

I tucked her hands neatly into her lap. I always do. It's a courtesy.

Then I let my fingers wander over the purse she dropped during the struggle. A beige, cheap thing with peeling vinyl and a half-broken zipper. Inside: car keys, two rosary beads tangled together, an old grocery receipt, a pack of gum, and a wrinkled family photo.

Two sons.

Both grown.

Both smiling like they'd never known fear.

I set the photo on her lap, ink-side up, facing her, as if she could still draw comfort from the faces she raised. Or maybe as a reminder that every life ends, no matter how many people you lived it for.

Blood smeared across one boy's cheek where my thumb brushed it.

Accidental.

But I didn't fix it.

A message doesn't need words to be understood.

My mother kept a rosary just like this one in her glove compartment. Said it kept the car safe. It never kept her safe, but I still think of her hands when I see the beads.

The stairs below were splattered with red from her attempt to escape, a sloppy breadcrumb trail of desperation. I stepped around it, not out of fear of leaving prints, but out of respect for the pattern. I liked the shape her terror made. Wide arcs. Sudden stops. Perfect little heel-slides where her shoes lost traction.

A map of her fear.

I took one last look at her. Head bowed. Eyes gone. Ears gone. Tongue gone. Everything she used to survive this world stripped clean. Everything she used to resist me removed.

"See no evil," I murmured.

The lights flickered. The stairwell buzzed. A car alarm chirped faintly somewhere below.

I pressed my hand to her shoulder, not affection, not comfort, just acknowledgment. Then I let her fall sideways onto the landing, her body folding like a marionette with cut strings. Legs bent. Arm twisted under. Face pointed toward the stairwell door like she was waiting for help that would never come.

I stood over her a moment longer.

Then I left.

Slow.

Quiet.

Leaving her for someone who would never forget what they saw.

Monsters don't need to roar to be heard.

Sometimes we only have to whisper.

CHAPTER
TWENTY-THREE

NIKO

Rose was already pacing when I walked in.

I closed the door gently, like maybe that would soften the weight I was dragging behind me. It didn't.

She didn't look at me when she spoke. "You're spiraling."

Straight to it.

"I'm doing my job."

"No," she said, turning with her arms crossed, "you're chasing a ghost."

"It's not a ghost," I snapped. "It's Dante. He's out there."

"And what happens when you catch him?" she asked. "You think it'll bring your dad back? Think it'll fix everything?"

"I didn't say that."

"You didn't have to."

I sighed and dropped into the armchair. My jacket still smelled like the stairwell. Blood and bleach and whatever perfume the woman wore before she died.

Rose stayed standing. That used to mean she was trying to stay strong for me. Lately it felt like she was bracing for the next impact.

"I'm close," I said finally. "This last victim... there was a photo in her bag. Two sons. Smiling. Happy."

Rose's expression softened for a heartbeat.

"He staged it," I continued. "Set the photo in her lap. Her blood was on it. It wasn't random. He wanted us to see it."

She stared at me, lips parted like she had something to say but wasn't sure if it would land as concern or accusation. Finally she asked, "And what did you see?"

I felt the answer claw its way up my throat, something raw and ugly, and for a second, I couldn't breathe. The photo wasn't just evidence. It had weight. Shape. A pulse. As if touching it had put something in me I couldn't quite shake. I hesitated longer than I meant to, because saying it out loud felt like handing it power.

I looked down at my hands. I didn't want to answer.

Because the truth was, I saw myself. Just for a second. In the blood. In the quiet. In the fact that I didn't flinch.

"He's taunting us," I said instead. "And I'm going to make him stop."

Rose crossed the room and knelt in front of me. Her hands were warm on mine, grounding in a way I didn't deserve.

"I need you to come back to me, Niko," she whispered. "Before there's nothing left."

Her voice trembled on the last word, and it gutted me. Not because she thought I was dangerous—because she thought I was disappearing.

So I nodded.

And lied through my teeth.

———

We were back in the bullpen.

Same shitty fluorescents. Same chipped whiteboard. Same empty coffee pot no one had refilled since the last body dropped. It felt wrong to drink caffeine when someone's eyes were missing.

DJ was slumped in his chair, fingers pinching the bridge of his nose. Caz was pacing again, muttering under her breath like each footstep might stomp out the unease curling between us.

For a moment I almost didn't pull it out. The image still clung to me, sticky as the blood smeared across it. Part of me wanted to hide it, to pretend I hadn't felt whatever I felt staring at it. But the truth was already under my skin.

I slapped a printout on the table.

"Photo was found in her lap. Family. Two sons. Killer smeared one of their faces, just enough blood to look accidental. It wasn't."

DJ looked up. "What are we supposed to take from that?"

"He's sending a message," I said. "No one's off-limits. Not the innocent. Not the loved ones. Not even the memory of safety."

Caz snorted. "You think this is about memories now?"

"I think it's about fear. And control. And symbolism. He's not just killing. He's curating."

"Creepy-ass curator," Caz added. "Next thing you know he'll start signing his work."

I ignored the urge to smile.

She stopped pacing. "Okay, preacher. What's the sermon?"

I gestured at the board. Three names now. My father. Toby. Denise Hardin.

"He escalated after the prison break," I said. "No pattern at first. But now the presentation is sharpening. Toby was brutal but sloppy. Denise was clinical again. He's adapting."

DJ leaned back. "So you're saying what? He's regaining control?"

"I'm saying we need to treat him like someone ten steps ahead, not like a wild animal that chewed through a fence."

Caz shook her head. "So what, we sit around waiting for the next body? Hope he leaves a diary?"

"No," I said. "We change the game."

I reached into my jacket and pulled out a folded notepad. "I spoke to a witness yesterday. Gas station clerk. Maya Sloan. She said she's seen Dante."

That actually stops Caz.

"Wait, what?"

"She recognized him from the news. Thinks she saw him two or three times last week. Never up close, but always nearby. Always watching."

"Why didn't you say that sooner?" DJ asked.

"Because I didn't want to jump the gun. People lie. People get scared. But I looked her in the eye. She wasn't lying."

"And now she's on his radar," Caz muttered.

I nodded. "Which means she needs protection."

"Twenty-four hour surveillance?" DJ asked.

"Yeah. Rotate shifts. No room for error."

Caz grabbed a marker and wrote on the board, underlined three times:

MAYA SLOAN – PRIORITY

"Great," she said. "Another person we have to babysit while Satan's scrapbooker plays peekaboo with body parts. Anyone else know?"

"Not yet. Just us. I didn't want her name floating until we could lock her down."

"Smart," DJ said, though his tone was worn. "But if he knows we're onto her—"

"Then he's already making his move."

The bullpen went quiet again. Even the air felt still.

I stared at the board. My father's face watched from the top corner. Beneath it, two more photos. Two more deaths. All connected by one man.

CHAPTER
TWENTY-FOUR
DANTE

I always preferred to follow in silence.

Not because I was afraid of being seen. But because I wanted to see. Everything. The way they walked. The weight in their limbs. The invisible rituals people performed when they believed they were alone.

Calvin Ross checked his reflection every time he passed glass. He didn't notice the limp in his left leg, the one that started after the accident five years ago. But I noticed. I counted the extra second it took him to step down curbs. I tracked the way his shoulder dipped when he was tired. The way his jacket always bunched at the collar. He never learned to dress himself without her.

She left him. I remember that. Right after the promotion he didn't deserve.

He parked in the same garage every night, level 3C, back row. Liked the corner space. Less chance of someone dinging the leased Audi. Didn't like people near him. Or maybe he just didn't like people.

I watched from across the street as he left work. It was after eight. He was late, probably stayed behind to print out numbers he didn't understand. He always thought spreadsheets were strategy.

He didn't see me. No one did.

I followed at a distance. Not close enough to draw suspicion, not far enough to lose him. Just close enough to memorize.

He grabbed Skyline Chili for dinner. Extra napkins. Ate in his car with the windows up, chewing with his mouth open while scrolling through news he didn't read.

There was something almost pathetic about him now.

Not the kind of pathetic that earned mercy.

The kind that earned erasure.

He didn't know his name had already been chosen. That he was already circling the drain and calling it routine.

Tomorrow.

Maybe the next day.

I hadn't decided.

But I would.

And when I did, I wondered if he'd recognize me.

Probably not.

He never looked past the surface.

After I chose him, the world slowed down, not in the cinematic way people romanticize, but in a quieter, interior way. Like my blood started moving softer. Like the clatter of conscience finally stopped. Like all that was left was breath and bone and purpose.

I watched Calvin through windows, across sidewalks, behind tinted glass. The kind of watching that feels like prayer, or hunger, or both. He moves like a man unburdened. Like someone who forgot. Like someone who never once considered the past might catch up to him with teeth.

I didn't feel anything yet. Not hatred, not joy, not even anticipation.

What I felt was rightness.

The clean fit of a knife returning to its sheath. The click of a lock meeting the exact shape of its key. The certainty that this was always going to happen, and I was simply walking the long, necessary path to get here.

Maybe I'd give him a final cruelty: letting him die confused. Letting him die thinking it was random. Letting him die without the dignity of understanding why.

I imagined the scene. The precision. The blood. The art of it.

They'd analyze it like the rest. DJ would lean in, squint, call it structured. Caz would drop a joke to keep from trembling. And Niko, Niko would look a second too long at the symmetry like it was whispering something he almost remembered.

He'd say, "Calvin never struck me as a guy who scared easy," like it was nothing. Like he didn't know.

But he did know.

Not all of it. Not yet. But somewhere beneath the parts of him still pretending, he knew this was personal.

That this was mine.

That it always was.

CHAPTER
TWENTY-FIVE

NIKO

The body was waiting for us.

Front steps of the precinct. Just outside the double doors. Slumped like someone left a drunk to sleep it off. But the blood told a different story.

DJ was the first to spot it. He stopped mid-sentence, went still, and slammed the brakes on his own breath.

Caz drew her weapon with a muttered, "Oh, fuck me."

And I... I just stared.

Calvin Ross. Mouth open like it caught the scream too late. Throat opened clean and cruel, like the blade knew exactly where to kiss him. His eyes were gone. Ears too. Tongue a mangled mess in his lap.

Same surgical ritual. Same message.

He was here.

But this time, there was an actual message.

Written across Calvin's shirt in dried brown-red strokes, dragged by a trembling finger or maybe the edge of a tongue before it was cut loose:

DJ crouched to confirm the obvious. "Yep. Dante. Same... everything."

Caz stepped back, pinching the bridge of her nose. "At least he's saving us the trouble of driving. If he kills one of us, maybe he'll just wheel us inside."

"Don't joke," DJ muttered.

"I'm not," she said. "That was me manifesting boundaries."

I couldn't look away.

Not from Calvin.

Not from what was left of him. He was just another piece of meat on the killer's cutting board.

I swallowed hard and heard myself say it aloud:

"Calvin never struck me as a guy who scared easy."

Nobody responded.

Not right away.

Caz broke the silence first. "Guess even the tough ones scream when you start pulling out their tongue."

DJ flinched. "Jesus."

"What? You think this guy's playing nice now?" She gestured at the body. "We're past subtle."

And she was right.

This wasn't escalation anymore.

This was performance.

Public, precise, punishing.

Fucking Dante. He wanted us rattled.

He wanted it close and personal.

And it was.

Because Calvin knew him.

And I couldn't shake the feeling that the noose was tightening around both our necks.

———

Maya met me at LaRosa's. Pizza was the comfort food we all needed right now. It was half past nine. She was early, fidgeting with her sleeve, bouncing her knee under the table like she was trying to outrun her nerves.

Something in me tightened at the sight. Too young. Too worn down. Too alone.

It hit me faster than I liked—that instinctive flare in my chest, protective and sharp, like my body had decided she was already under my watch whether I understood why or not.

I nodded to her before sliding into the booth.

She eyed the people walking in behind me. "You brought backup?"

"Technically," I said. "They're the good kind of backup."

DJ gave a small wave. "Hi."

Caz dropped into the booth beside Maya and grinned wide. "Bad kind's on vacation this week."

Maya stared. "Who... what kind of cop sits next to a civilian instead of across?"

"I like to keep people guessing," Caz said. "Besides, you looked like you might bolt. This way I get to use my stunning charm to keep you seated."

"I don't think that's what charm means," Maya mumbled.

DJ sat across from them, and I took the far edge, so we were boxed in like some twisted family dinner.

"Maya," I started gently, "we need to talk."

"I figured," she said. "You sounded like a sad funeral bell on the phone."

"She's not wrong," DJ muttered.

I slid a photo across the table. Not the body, just the shirt. The writing.

JUSTICE IS MINE

Her hand flinched before she touched the edge.

"We found him this morning," I said. "Calvin Ross."

Her eyes went wide. "What the fuck... Who is this?"

"One of Dante's old friends."

"Jesus," she breathed, curling in on herself a little. "I shouldn't have said anything."

The fear in her voice punched deeper than I expected. Not just witness fear—survivor fear. The kind that sinks its claws in. Something old and dangerous in me locked around the thought: *not her. Not again. Not this kid.*

"No," I said quickly. "You should've. And you need to keep talking."

Caz leaned in, resting her chin on her hand. "Think of us like anxiety midwives. Helping you deliver the truth with minimal screaming."

Maya snorted and smothered it behind her sleeve. "You're, like, the weirdest cop I've ever met."

"I contain multitudes."

DJ sighed. "Please don't quote Walt Whitman again."

I refocused. "We're assigning you protection, Maya. Starting now. Twenty-four-hour detail. Rotation schedule. No exceptions."

Her mouth opened, closes. "That's... serious."

"That's dead serious."

Caz winced. "Oof. Bad phrasing."

I ignored her. "Maya. You said you saw Dante. More than once."

"Yeah," she said, voice shaky. "He was wearing a hoodie. Kept his head down. But I swear it was him. Just standing there, like he was waiting for someone who never came."

DJ frowned. "You sure it wasn't someone who looked like him?"

"I don't know what I saw," she said, "but I saw how he stands. How he smokes. How he scratches behind his ear when he's thinking."

Caz lifted her brows. "Okay. I believe you. But also, you just described, like, three of my exes."

Maya laughed. Not loud, just a short, cracked breath that sounds almost like relief.

"Listen," I said. "If it was him, he's watching you. We don't know why yet. But you're not alone anymore."

She went quiet again. Fiddled with the pulled thread of her sleeve. "You're really gonna put people outside my place?"

"Already did."

"And if he comes for me?"

Caz pulled a cigarette from her coat and popped it between her teeth. "Then he'll have a really bad day."

DJ nodded, calm and solid. "We'll keep you safe. And Caz, we are inside."

She sighed and tucked the cigarette away.

Maya blinked hard, then nods. "Jesus Christ. Okay. Just...

don't let me end up like Calvin. And get that cigarette back out, I think I need it."

Caz smiled and put an arm around her. "I knew I liked you."

I met Maya's eyes. "We won't let you end up like Calvin."

The promise tasted wrong on my tongue—too big, too fragile, too easy to break. And the way she looked at me, like I was the only barrier between her and whatever waited in the dark, made something in my chest clench hard.

But even as I said it, my stomach churned.

Because the killer knew Calvin.

He chose him.

And Maya?

She was officially on the list.

CHAPTER
TWENTY-SIX

DANTE

He flinched before the knife even touched him, and I think that was the moment I finally understood the truth of him. The softness under the swagger. The way time had worn down every edge he used to pretend he had. Calvin Ross was never brave. He just liked standing near brave people. Liked borrowing their shine, like a man who stands close to a fire and claims he struck the match.

Maybe that's why watching him now, seeing recognition bloom and curdle and twist into something primal, felt almost holy.

He opened the door only halfway, the chain lock dangling uselessly. For a long second he didn't speak. Didn't blink. Just stared at me like he was looking at a ghost wearing all the worst parts of him like a second skin.

He tried to smile. That old salesman grin. Cracked now, brittle as sun-damaged paint. Then he saw my knife.

"H-hey, man," he stammered, "I told you everything—"

I stepped inside before he finished the lie.

His breath hitched.

There.

The flinch.

Once you hear the sound of a man's courage breaking, you never mistake it for anything else. He backed up fast, bumping the table, knocking over dusty takeout boxes he never threw away. A photo frame fell and clattered across the hardwood—his ex-wife and their dog, smiling like the world was worth trusting.

He tried to run down the hall. I let him. Let him believe distance could save him. His footsteps slapped the floor, sloppy and wild, like his body was trying to abandon him.

I caught up easily.

I always do.

The first strike wasn't deep, just enough to cut through shirt and skin, enough to send him sprawling into the wall with a strangled gasp wrapped in disbelief and pain. He looked back at me with wide, watering eyes, like appealing to a shared memory could stop what was coming.

"Please... wait... don't—"

But he never waited for anyone.

Why should I?

He crawled, hands slipping in his own blood, knees dragging across the floor as if moving toward a light he didn't deserve. His breath rattled thin and quivering, the kind that tells you the lungs have already accepted what the mind refuses to understand.

I walked behind him slowly.

Not out of cruelty.

Out of certainty.

The second strike folded him forward. The third pinned

him to the floor. Then I straddled him gently, like comforting a dying friend, like giving him one last human touch before the world forgot him.

His hands trembled. Then he whispered a word—maybe "why," maybe a name, maybe a prayer—but the tongue is a slippery thing, and it lied even now, thick with desperation.

I took it first.

Then the ears.

Then the eyes.

Sometimes I switch the order, but this one always felt right: silence, blindness, truth.

His body relaxed at the end. They all do.

Death is the last exhale of a life that mattered less than it believed.

I sat with him a long time.

Longer than usual. Long enough to almost remember what he looked like when he still mattered.

I carried him through the city like a man escorting something sacred, his weight draped over my shoulder in a way that felt strangely familiar, as if I had done this in another life. The night was cold and sharp enough to cut through the stink of death clinging to us both.

The precinct rose from the concrete like a fortress that forgot what it was guarding.

Too bright.

Too busy.

Too sure of itself.

I approached from the east side, where the cameras

stutter and glitch, where the blind spot runs long enough for a man to disappear and reappear clean. The air tasted metallic, a rain that never fell.

Calvin's body thumped softly against my back.

Dead weight is honest.

Alive weight lies.

I lowered him on the top step with surprising gentleness. Kneeling, positioning, arranging his limbs, wiping the blood from his cheek only to smear it deliberately across his shirt. I straightened his collar. Smoothed the wrinkles. Closed his jaw. Opened his fingers.

He looked peaceful.

Peace is a lie, but it photographs well.

I wrote the message slowly.

Carefully.

With intention.

JUSTICE IS MINE

Three words.

All teeth.

Then I looked at him one last time. A man who spent his life taking credit he never earned. Now reduced to a message he never understood.

I walked away before the door opened.

Before the scream rose.

Before the world pretended to be shocked.

I didn't need to watch.

My work was done.

CHAPTER
TWENTY-SEVEN

NIKO

Rose found me outside, on the back steps of the precinct, one hand gripping a coffee cup that went cold hours ago.

I didn't hear her at first. Too busy staring into nothing, trying to piece together a puzzle that felt like it was made from different boxes.

"You haven't slept," she said gently. "Not even a nap."

I didn't respond.

She stepped closer, arms folded. "You're shaking. You need rest, Niko. This isn't sustainable."

That's when something sharp and ugly broke loose in me.

"I can't rest, Rose," I snapped. "Every time I close my eyes, I see their faces. My father. Toby. That woman in the stairwell with her fucking eyes gone. Calvin Ross—Jesus, he left him on our damn doorstep."

Her face hardened.

"I know what's happening, okay?" I pressed. "I'm close. I

can feel it. Something in this is shifting. He's not just killing anymore, he's sending a message. And if I back off now, if I let up for even a second, someone else dies."

"You think you're the only one who gives a damn?"

She stepped back. "You're not the only person who's hurting. You're not the only one haunted. But you are the one falling apart. And if you keep pushing like this, you're going to break, and you'll take the rest of us down with you."

Silence stretched. I tried to apologize, but the words felt hollow.

She turned and walked away before I could force anything out.

And for a split second, guilt cut through the anger.

And just like that, I was alone again.

I pulled my phone from my coat pocket.

No missed calls. No new alerts.

I opened my messages. Scroll. Find Maya.

> You okay? Need anything? I can swing by later. Just say the word.

I stared at the screen longer than I should.

Then I flicked to DJ.

> You around? Need some backup before I lose my shit.

No response. He was probably on Maya duty tonight.

Caz next.

> You up? I need a distraction. Or alcohol. Or both.

She FaceTimed me thirty seconds later.

Of course she did.

I answered, and instantly she filled the screen—sprawled across her bed, one knee tucked up, tank top slouched low on one side. A thin cloud of smoke curled past her lips as she exhaled slow and lazy, cigarette between two fingers like she was posing for a noir still. Her purple hair was messy, piled up with a pen jammed through it. Her eyes lit up when she saw me.

"Well damn, detective," she said, voice low and teasing. "You look like hell."

"You're the second person to say that tonight."

She grinned, took another drag, and gestured with the hand holding her smoke. The one with the red string on it. "Means it must be true."

Her tank was threadbare—a hacked-up band tee dropped so low that for the first time, I noticed the soft swell of her breasts. Full. Barely contained. One strap slid so far down her shoulder it was practically a suggestion. And when she shifted to grab her drink, they moved under the fabric in a way that short-circuited my entire fucking brain.

I blinked hard.

This was Caz. The foul-mouthed, sharp-jawed partner who once head-butted a suspect for spitting on her boots. She was always been one of the guys—my guy. But now?

Now I couldn't stop looking.

She noticed. Of course she did. Her eyebrow quirked mid-sip. "You good there, hotshot?"

I tore my eyes off the screen, embarrassed. "Yeah. Just... tired."

She blew out another lazy stream of smoke. "Uh huh."

We talked nonsense for a while—old cases, precinct gossip, the usual dumb shit. But there was a tension under it now, something warm and strange and disorienting.

And I knew why.

It wasn't because of her. It was because of Rose.

Because things with Rose felt like they were fading—and I was desperate for anything that feels alive.

The realization hit like a bruise: I shouldn't be looking at someone else while the person who loves me is breaking under the weight of me.

Still, when Caz smirked and called me "pretty boy," I didn't argue.

I just let it sit there.

"Don't do anything stupid," she said finally, the cigarette now a glowing stub in the ashtray.

Then softer: "And don't fucking die. Seriously."

I nodded. "Same to you."

We hung up, and I sat in the dark, screen still glowing, heartbeat off-kilter.

Something was shifting. In the case. In me.

And I didn't know which was more dangerous.

***

Caz beat me to the office the next morning. She was perched on the edge of my desk like it was hers, legs crossed, puffing on a vape she swore wasn't technically smoking. Maybe a Sunday like this won't be so bad.

"You still look like hell," she said, eyes dragging over me with a slow grin. "Didn't get your beauty sleep?"

"Didn't get any sleep," I muttered, dropping my bag and

collapsing into my chair. "Spent half the night on FaceTime with a chain-smoking lunatic in a low-cut tank top."

Her smile widened. "And yet here you are. Still breathing. Must not be that bad."

"You're a menace."

"Maybe," she shrugged, leaning forward just enough for me to catch the dip of her neckline—intentional. "But admit it. You like the company."

I didn't answer because the truth tasted like guilt—bitter, familiar, impossible to swallow.

She didn't need me to answer, though.

Before it could shift into something else, DJ strolled in with a coffee in each hand and a smug grin.

"I come bearing peace offerings," he said, handing Caz a cup and sliding mine across the desk.

She squinted at him. "You look suspiciously cheerful for a man who did the night shift."

He shrugged. "Maya's not so bad. Spitfire. We watched two true crime documentaries, played Uno, and she beat my ass at Mario Kart."

Caz barked a laugh. "That's our girl."

"She's sharp," DJ said. "I think she saw something she hasn't processed yet. But I kept it light."

"Good," I said. "Let her warm up. She's been through enough."

And then the moment died.

A rapid knock on the glass.

An officer stepped in, pale and sweating.

"You need to see this," he said. "Now."

The news was already on every screen.

Live footage. Fountain Square. Two dead.

A couple. Broad daylight. In the middle of the crowd.

He was there.

No names yet, but the images were everywhere—police tape wrapped around the fountain, anchors speaking in hushed tones reserved for mass tragedy.

Caz went silent. DJ's jaw clenched. My hands went cold.

This wasn't hidden.

This was a statement.

The killer wasn't hiding anymore. And the whole damn city was watching.

We killed the audio, but the video looped behind us, blurring into background noise:

Blood in the square. Yellow tape like streamers. A city-wide panic party and we're the unwilling hosts.

Caz sank into the nearest chair, barely able to with her curvy body. DJ leaned against the evidence board, arms crossed, knuckles white.

I stared at the wall of faces—Toby, the paralegal, Calvin. Now two more would join them.

Strangers, carved up for spectacle.

"We need to build the pattern," I said. My voice was hoarse but steady. "If this was personal, we missed it. If it's random, we missed that too. Either way, he's winning."

Caz straightened. "So what do we know?"

DJ started pacing. "Victim one: Tony. Emotional. Messy. Two: Toby. Controlled. Almost surgical. Three: Paralegal in a stairwell. Clean signature. Four: Calvin. Left on our doorstep. Five and six—" he gestured at the screen "—full-blown performance art."

"Maybe Dante grew up," Caz said quietly. "Maybe this is what grown-up rage looks like."

"No," I said. "It's something else. It's dispassionate. Like he's proving a point and we're too slow to catch it."

I grabbed a marker and drew a thin red line through each photo—looping them like beads on a rosary. A prayer we couldn't finish.

"Target types vary. Gender varies. Public versus private varies. What doesn't vary?"

"Signature," DJ said. "The removal. Eyes, ears, tongue."

"Control," Caz added. "Every scene feels calm. Even the public ones. No chaos. Just silence."

"So what's he saying?" I asked. "What's the message?"

No one answered.

We didn't know.

But we stayed in that room for two hours. No breaks. No bullshit.

Mapping timelines. Re-checking statements. Digging through Dante's old files. Trying to outrun a pattern that already had momentum.

We moved names. Added pins. Redrew lines.

And somewhere in the middle of it, Caz pinned a sticky note beside Calvin's photo:

JUSTICE IS MINE

She underlined it twice, hard enough to wrinkle the paper.

"Then let's take it back," she said.

CHAPTER
TWENTY-EIGHT
DANTE

I saw them leave The Banks just as the sun was coming up for the day, its light was gray and lazy, unable to decide if it was retreating or rising. The crowd was thinning, the riverfront buzz shifting toward pre-game chaos. I trailed them with ease, two people who believed they were invisible or at least safe. Saturday was finished, and Sunday was here.

She wore a pale coat, mid-thirties, hair loose and catching the breeze off the riverfront. He was taller, broad shouldered, sleeves cuffed, tie undone. He looked like a man about to shed his day job for something duller and quieter. They laughed once, short bursts, the kind you hear in the margins of a city's rush. They had no idea.

They passed the bars and the riverwalk lights, slipped between the crowds and the streetcar tracks, and I stayed two shadows behind.

When they changed direction toward Fountain Square, I slowed. Let the square open up around them. People standing. Bengals fans clustering. Tourists snapping photos. Families with kids and dogs. Noise. Light. Life.

Then they sat on the edge of the fountain, an act of casual romance in the middle of everything. He tossed a coin in. She leaned her head on his shoulder. The fountain overflowed in bronze shadows. A bubble of something sacred and human.

I crouched behind a column, gaze sliding across the cracked stone steps, water dripping, neon signs reflecting off the surface like fractured glass.

Perfect.

He turned and pointed at the fountain's sculpture, the Tyler Davidson Fountain, something he said reminded him of home. She laughed, small and real.

The moment stretched.

And then I moved closer.

Not touching yet.

Just closing the gap so they could feel it, whatever *it* was, then wonder where I was hiding.

He didn't see me. She didn't. They believed in ordinary morning, in stolen time, in warmth. I believed in justice. In revenge. In reclamation.

Something inside me shifted. Rightness. The knife's edge. The waiting. The knowing.

I stepped into the light for a second, just enough for a shadow to cross his view, but he looked away. Only her eyes flicked up. Only hers caught that flicker.

The world didn't stop. The fountain kept spilling. The crowd kept laughing.

But I felt the pull in her, just a fraction of fear, before it vanished.

The square was my stage now—an audience too busy living their own lives to notice the play unfolding around them. Thousands of eyes, and not one looking where it mattered.

They rose from the fountain the way all soft, ordinary people do, slowly and lazily, not yet aware they were walking toward the end of their story. He checked his phone. She smoothed her coat. A moment so painfully human it almost felt like a warning.

But warnings only matter to the living.

I stayed two bodies behind, letting the crowd move like water around us. Early tailgaters drifting toward bars. Parents bribing kids with cocoa. The hum of the fountain turning everything into a lullaby.

He answered a call. She wandered toward the shaded row of tables under the Fifth Third awning, looking for a trash can, alone just long enough.

Opportunity blooms like a bruise.

She stopped on the steps, fumbling with her coffee lid.

That was all I needed.

I was behind her before she turned, one hand clamped over her mouth, the other sliding a thin blade between her ribs, angled up, fast, silent. Her gasp died against my palm. Her knees buckled. I guided her down gently, easing her into sleep, her breath spilling through my fingers in fading bursts.

It took six seconds.

No more.

Her body was light, easier to move than I expected. I dragged her behind a stack of unused patio chairs, hidden from the square by columns and the morning glare. Shadows swallowed her completely.

The man didn't notice at first. He finished his call, scanned the crowd, and laughed at something no one else heard. Then he saw her coffee cup on the ground, upright but trembling with wind.

He walked toward it. I stepped behind a column, letting him pass me, so close I could smell his cologne, something cheap meant to smell expensive. He knelt to pick up the cup, confusion blooming on his face, and that was when I let the shadow fall over him.

He turned.

I gripped the back of his head and slammed it once into the stone column, the crack sharp like fireworks too close to the ear. His body sagged, stunned, and I used the moment to slip the blade under his jawline, deep and precise, warm red spilling down his shirt. He gurgled once, breath catching on instinct, then nothing.

He joined her beside the chairs, two bodies curled into each other like they had chosen it.

The real work began after.

I checked my watch, forty seconds, maybe fifty before anyone wandered too close.

Plenty.

I knelt and began with the eyes.

Theirs had gone glassy already, pupils blown wide, seeing nothing. The first cut is always the easiest, a careful slide beneath, lift, twist. The second eye comes free smoother, like the flesh has surrendered.

I moved to the ears next. Small, delicate, useless little petals, severed with two practiced strokes each.

Then the tongues.

Both taken with a quick, sure technique: one hand to open the jaw, the blade angled down, a single decisive cut. They always look surprised, even in death. As if they never imagined silence could be carved into them.

Behind me, the crowd laughed at something—a Bengals chant starting, someone shouting about beer prices. No one turned. No one noticed.

Bodies arranged. Heads tilted toward the fountain as if admiring it.

As if listening.

I stepped back.

A breeze moved through the square, lifting the woman's hair in a soft sweep. It looked almost tender.

Almost.

Then I disappeared into the crowd like a ripple folding into the river of the city. Unseen, untroubled, unhurried.

Justice is mine.

And I would give it again.

And again.

And again.

CHAPTER
TWENTY-NINE

NIKO

Dante wasn't spiraling.

He was orchestrating.

Every time we thought we were catching up, he was already somewhere else—three turns ahead, hands clean, eyes watching. Calvin's body hadn't even gone cold before the news hit about the couple at Fountain Square. Brazen. Precise. Timed like clockwork. A fucking spectacle.

It was past midnight when I finally sat down. Not home. Not with Rose. Just... down. On a bench outside the precinct, elbows on my knees, staring at the sidewalk like it might offer answers. My back ached. My thoughts felt splintered. My skin felt tight. I'd been running on rage and instinct so long I was starting to forget what calm even was.

Caz said something earlier about sleep.

She joked, but it wasn't the good kind. It sounded cracked underneath. I filed it away—one more thing shoved into the corners of my head, pretending it doesn't weigh a ton.

I pulled up the crime board on my phone—zoomed in on the photo DJ took before they zipped Calvin into the bag.

JUSTICE IS MINE

Written in his blood. Not rushed. Not messy. Just... decided.

It didn't make sense.

None of it did.

Toby. Denise. The couple. No thread that holds in daylight. No motive that fit.

Except Dante.

And even that felt thin now.

My eyes stung. I rubbed them hard, like I could scrape out the exhaustion. Didn't help.

I checked in on Maya. Just a text. She replied fast. Said DJ was nice. Said she felt safer with us around. I lied and told her we were close.

We weren't.

But I had to believe we were getting there.

I had to.

The house was dim—just the blue haze of the TV flickering across the walls. Rose was on the couch, curled under a blanket, staring at a show she wasn't watching. No sound. Just the hum of everything we weren't saying.

"Hey," I murmured.

Nothing.

I took off my shoes, set my keys down gently. Tried to

move carefully, like maybe that would fix something. She didn't look at me when I sat beside her. Didn't flinch.

"I didn't mean to be gone that long," I said. "I got caught up—"

"Don't," she cut in, voice flat. "You always get caught up."

That stung more than I wanted to admit. I leaned forward, elbows on my knees. "You know I'm trying to stop him. You saw the report."

"I see everything, Niko. You leave the files on the table, on the fridge, in the bathroom. I see every fucking photo, every fucking headline, every fucking piece of someone who's never coming home again."

Silence.

She turned toward me now, finally, but her eyes were harder than they used to be. Tired. Sharp.

"I used to be scared you'd get hurt," she said. "Now I'm just scared you're not coming back at all. Even when you walk through that door."

I didn't know what to say to that. Not really.

"I can't stop," I whispered. "Not when we're this close. Not when people are dying in the middle of the fucking city."

"I'm not asking you to stop," she snaps. "I'm asking if there's anything left of you under all of this. Because I don't recognize you anymore."

I stood, pacing. Anger bubbled up—not at her, but at me, at Dante, at the case, at time itself. "You think I want to be this way? You think I like drowning in it?"

"I think you don't care what it's doing to us."

That's when it landed. The "us" sounded foreign coming

out of her mouth, like a language we hadn't spoken in weeks.

I sat back down. My voice softened. "I do care. I'm just… I'm losing my grip, Ro. If I stop moving, I'll fall apart."

What I didn't say—what lodged in my throat like a splinter—was that sometimes I wasn't sure the falling apart would stop. That maybe Dante had carved something loose inside me the day he killed my father, and every body since had widened the crack.

She stared at me, long and cold. Then she got up.

"Then maybe fall," she said, walking to the bedroom. "Because I'm tired of being the only one holding you together."

The door shut behind her.

And I was left in the quiet.

Still in my coat.

Still carrying blood that wasn't mine.

Still chasing a ghost who used to be a man I thought I knew.

THIRTY

DANTE

I sat with my blade across my knee like a prayer, the steel resting against my thigh and catching the morning light through the blinds. Streaked in blood from yesterday, arterial and warm and human, it had already cooled and hardened, turned to a film like drying lacquer.

Cleaning it wasn't just a chore. It was a ritual.

Each swipe of the cloth was a memory pulled tight, a frame-by-frame still of the woman's scream catching in her throat. They died believing they were just coincidence. That amused me more than it should have.

I angled the cloth between the serrated edge, careful not to nick myself. This wasn't clumsiness work. This was craft. You don't chip marble with a hammer. You sculpt. You worship the form beneath the mess.

Blood in the teeth of the blade. Gum tissue, maybe. Something pink and fibrous.

I ran the cloth slower now. Gentle. Reverent.

This blade had taken many souls already. It had silenced

voices that thought they mattered. It had learned what it meant to unmake a face, to peel back the symbols of identity until nothing remained but bone and memory.

I didn't name it. I wasn't that dramatic.

But I knew it better than I knew myself.

There were fingerprints on the hilt from the first night I used it. I never wiped them off. Not because I was sloppy, but because I wanted to remember who I was before. The man with trembling hands and hesitation in his breath. He didn't exist anymore.

I cleaned around those prints, preserved them like fossils.

When the blade was finally clean, I set it down on the cloth like it was sleeping.

I would remember those two. The daylight was a rush.

This wasn't rage. This was order. This was the consequence of forgetting.

And I was here to remind them.

One body at a time.

CHAPTER
THIRTY-ONE

NIKO

Caz met me outside before I could come in and start my next shift.

She dropped onto the bench beside mine. No file. No hello. Just her usual heat and a cup of something that smelled better than the sludge I'd been drinking.

"Something's off," she said, low.

I didn't look up. "You mean besides everything?"

"The couple. Fountain Square. It's not like the others."

I stayed quiet.

"No message. No cleanup either. Just clean, fast, public."

Still didn't look at her.

She leaned in closer. Her arm grazed mine, just barely, but enough to register. She was smoking again even though the signs said not to. Smoke curled across the space between us, soft and slow like it had time to kill.

"Maybe he's losing control," she said.

"Or maybe he's getting cocky."

"Or maybe," she said, dragging the last syllable out like

she was tasting it, "he's changing the rules just to fuck with you."

I looked at her then. Her shirt was unbuttoned just enough to make me notice. Not obscene. Not subtle either. Her smirk was smug. She saw the glance, and she liked it.

I looked away first.

And the guilt came a beat later—sharp, stupid, perfectly timed. I shouldn't have noticed. Not with Rose barely speaking to me. Not with the world cracking open under our feet. But exhaustion makes you reckless, and loneliness makes everything so much worse.

"We need to go back over everything," I said. "Build the pattern. Or figure out why it's breaking."

She took one last drag off her cigarette and smushed it out in my empty mug, grazing her breasts across my arm. Was that intentional? I was only noticing because Rose was distant.

"Sure thing, boss," she said, standing. "Just don't go crazy on me."

We walked into the precinct side by side. Not together, exactly. Just in sync.

I was still replaying our conversation, Caz's words about patterns and fear and the stupid heat in my chest when she leaned in, when I saw Maya sitting at the front desk.

Legs crossed. Jacket too big. Coffee in one hand, phone in the other. She looked like she claimed the station as her own.

The second she spotted us, she grinned.

"Well, well, well," she called out, loud enough for heads to turn. "Look who finally decided to show their face after sneaking out on me this morning."

Caz didn't miss a beat. "You were snoring like a freight train. I figured if I stayed, I'd never sleep again."

Maya gasped, hand to her chest. "Excuse me, I purr when I sleep."

"You hiss like a raccoon in a trash fire."

I kept walking and didn't even try to hide the smirk.

Maya pointed at me as I passed. "You gonna let her talk to me like that, Niko?"

"I'm staying out of this."

"Smart man," Caz said. "That's why he's still alive."

Maya rolled her eyes but laughed anyway. "I just came to say thanks for last night. She was great, actually. Protective. Surprisingly charming."

"You told me to fake nice," Caz muttered.

"Yeah, but you faked it so well. I almost believed you liked me."

"Don't push it."

They were ridiculous. But I let them go at it for another few lines of banter while I grabbed the case files from the front desk. DJ was late. Rose hadn't texted back. And I was trying not to think about either of those things.

Eventually Maya turned to me, serious for half a breath. "You're sure this 24/7 thing is necessary?"

I nodded. "Until we know for sure what you saw, yeah. It is."

She exhaled. "Then I guess I'll get used to my new body-guard girlfriend."

Caz tossed an arm around her shoulder. "Damn right you will."

The door buzzed behind us.

DJ stepped in, hoodie pulled low, fast food bag in one

hand and a black coffee in the other. His eyes scanned the lobby, paused when he saw me, then flicked to Caz and Maya standing close.

"You two start dating while I was off-duty, or what?"

Maya grinned. "Jealous?"

Caz rolled her eyes. "No. He's terrified."

DJ dropped the bag on the nearest desk with a thud. "Nothing can terrify me when I have my sausage biscuits."

I raised an eyebrow. "How was the night?"

He sipped the coffee first. "Good, actually. Maya's energy is all over the place, but she didn't try to kill me, so I'm calling it a win."

Maya gave him a two-finger salute. "Only because you snore quieter than she does."

"I do not snore," DJ and Caz said at the same time, then looked at each other and groaned.

I took the case files from under my arm and tapped them against the edge of the desk. "Glad you two didn't kill each other. We're gonna need the help. Things are getting worse."

"Yeah," DJ said, his tone dropping. "We need to find Dante now. Especially after that couple..."

I nodded.

Maya froze. "Wait, what couple?"

"Later," I told her. "Not now."

She didn't look convinced.

Caz caught my glance. "We'll fill you in once we get to the board."

DJ took another bite of his biscuit. "You know, when I signed up for homicide, I didn't think I'd need to brush up on urban crowd dismemberment."

Caz clapped him on the back. "Welcome to Cincinnati."

I was about to drag everyone toward the board when the squad room doors swung open again and our coworker Paige Marshall stepped inside with a bakery box the size of a small child.

"Morning," she called, lifting it just enough to show off the logo. "Treats for whoever hasn't had sleep or joy in the last seventy-two hours."

DJ groaned dramatically. "Of course you bring donuts on the one day I actually pack my own breakfast."

Paige smirked. "Tragic. But I believe in balance."

Caz perked up. "Fuck yeah. You keeping us from a sugar crash or trying to bribe us?"

"Why not both?" Paige popped the lid, and half the room drifted toward her like she'd summoned them.

Caz took a powdered one, eyed her over the rim. "So, when are you introducing us to your new guy? Evan, right? The AI nerd?"

Paige made a face. "He's not a nerd."

Caz raised an eyebrow. Paige sighed.

"Okay, he's a nerd. But he's my nerd. Mostly."

Caz snorted. "God help him."

Paige shot her a playful glare. "Eat your donut and behave."

I grabbed a chocolate one out of the box on instinct, mostly to avoid getting dragged into their nonsense, and nodded toward the evidence board.

"Alright. Donuts are fine, but let's get to work now."

Paige gave me a mock salute. "Yes, Detective. Try not to ruin everyone's morning before the sugar hits."

And just like that, she was swallowed by the noise of the precinct, another moving part in the chaos.

THIRTY-TWO

DANTE

She wasn't like the others.

Most of them walked through the world on autopilot. Distracted. Confident in systems that never protected them to begin with. They talked loud, laughed harder, flashed badges like armor. But not her.

She watched.

Not always with her eyes, she was too smart for that.

Sometimes I almost admired that. The discipline. The hunger tucked beneath her smirk. Most people sleepwalk through danger, but she moved as if she'd already survived something worse.

She watched with her timing, her silences, the way her shoulders shifted when she sensed the perimeter changing. She listened to what wasn't said. She noticed what didn't belong.

And something in her had started turning.

I saw it in the way she lingered at the scene too long. The way her fingers hovered over a missing connection like she could almost touch it. The way her lips twisted, not in confusion but in recognition.

They didn't know I was always watching.

She didn't know what she knew yet. But it was there. In the corners. In the cracks between conclusions. A tension forming beneath the surface, tightening with every step I took.

She was starting to understand that this wasn't chaos. That the blood had rhythm. That the message had structure. That I had been leading them somewhere, one corpse at a time.

And she was close to hearing the music.

Too close.

I felt it when her tone changed, when the jokes came with shorter edges, when the spaces between her words were weighted with something less playful. When she brushed off certainty like it was starting to itch.

If she kept digging, she'd find me.

If she kept listening, she'd hear what the others couldn't.

But she wouldn't stop.

That was the problem with instincts like hers, they didn't just fade. They calcified. Hardened into obsession. And once that happened, there was only one cure.

She'd see it soon enough. She'd try to name it, try to warn them.

But by then it'd be too late.

She was already marked.

Not because she was weak.

Because she was right.

And nobody got to be right forever.

CHAPTER
THIRTY-THREE

NIKO

The laughter faded fast when I pulled up the close-ups.

Victim 1: Henry Miles, 36. Lived in Oakley, worked at a bank. He and his wife had two kids.

Victim 2: His wife, Sophia Miles, 34. Photographer, studio in Covington. No history with Dante. No obvious reason to die in the middle of the goddamn city.

Maya scanned the crime board. Slower this time. No more jokes. Just a narrowing of her eyes.

"We're sure they were random?" she asked.

I nodded.

"Could be symbolic," DJ muttered. "Fountain Square. Public. Daytime. Big screw-you to the whole city."

"Could be misdirection," Caz added, arms folded. "Make it look random when it's actually pointed."

"Toward me?" Maya asked.

No one answered.

She didn't like that.

I stepped in. "We can't confirm that yet. But you're staying under protection."

"Like hell," she scoffed.

"Maya," I said, low and sharp. "Humor me. Please."

She didn't argue. Just crossed her arms and studied the photos again. "How'd he manage to do that without anyone seeing? Eyes, tongue, ears. All that, and no one noticed?"

I shook my head. "Precision. He knew the moment. The angles. Probably waited for the noise to spike. There's a lot of water, motion, flashing lights. A scream would've just blended in."

DJ pulled up footage. It was choppy, a blur of bodies. But you could see the aftermath. Two people slumped. No one noticed for a solid minute. Then chaos.

Maya stared.

"Jesus," she whispered.

Caz leaned close to her. "Still wanna be involved?"

"I never said I wanted to," Maya muttered. "I just am."

She didn't flinch, didn't back down. That scared me more than anything.

I dragged my palm down my face and turned toward the board.

Photos. Notes. The couple. Calvin. Denise. All of it. We were building a map of grief.

"You're still thinking this is Dante?" Maya asked softly.

Caz answered for me. "We know it is. The how is still the problem."

"And the why," DJ added. "We don't know what the endgame is."

I stared at the fountain photo again. The bronze sculpture. Water mid-spill. Her head on his shoulder.

I couldn't shake that line. It wasn't a random kill. It was an execution staged with intention.

"He obviously doesn't care that we know it's him," I finally said. "He wants us to."

The silence stretched.

Then Caz let out a slow breath and slapped the board with the back of her hand. "Alright, folks. Time to build a profile. Stack the inconsistencies. Pull his patterns apart like taffy and find the weak spot."

Caz watched Maya walk toward the back room, then turned to me.

"Hey." She nudged my arm with the back of her knuckle. "Let me see your case notes."

I didn't look up. "They're a mess."

"You say that every time and then act surprised when I find patterns in your chicken scratch."

"I'll clean them up later."

She stared at me. Didn't move.

"Come on, Russo. I'm not trying to steal your thunder, I just..." Her tone softened. "I know how you get when you're this deep. And you missed a couple things on the Calvin board."

"I didn't miss anything."

"Okay," she said slowly, hands up like she was backing away from a wild animal. "Just saying. Double-checking is kind of my thing."

I finally looked up, tired and sharp. "I said I'll get to it."

The second the words left my mouth, I choked on the regret Not that I let it show. I just swallowed it and kept staring at the board like it deserved the blame.

Caz blinked at me, expression unreadable. Then she

shrugged like it was no big deal, but the tension stayed in her jaw.

"Alright, cowboy," she said, voice light but a little too measured. "But don't come crying to me when your brilliant theories fall apart in front of the mayor."

I let the silence hang.

She grabbed her coffee from the desk and turned to walk off, tossing one last line over her shoulder.

"Guess I'll just go flirt with Maya again. At least she appreciates my brilliance."

I almost smiled. Almost.

But the weight was still there. In the notes. In the board. In the back of my mind, scratching louder than ever.

Something was shifting. Caz felt it.

So did I.

CHAPTER
THIRTY-FOUR

DANTE

The rhythm came slower now. Measured. A controlled cadence I didn't always possess. I used to gasp after. Chest tight, jaw clenched, fingers buzzing like they were filled with light and couldn't hold it. Now, it's different. I breathe in through my nose—deep, steady, smooth like a tide pulling in—and I feel the air fill my chest with something like calm. Almost reverence. Almost grace.

It was strange, the stillness after blood. You'd expect panic. Regret. Some inner shaking that forces you to reckon with what you've done. But that's the myth. The delusion people cling to when they try to humanize monsters. They want the aftermath to ache.

But it didn't. Not for me.

There was just this quiet. This simplicity. This moment where my body hummed like a well-tuned instrument, every part of me aligned—present, finally, completely, undeniably here.

The blade was warm when I set it down. Not from the

metal. From me. From the friction of movement, the slick drag of muscle, the final slice. I stared at it now—how it caught the light in soft glints like a mirror made of memory.

My breath didn't hitch.

It didn't race.

It followed the pattern I'd trained into it—four seconds in, hold for four, exhale slow through the mouth for six. It was what I used to do before carving people up, when I had to focus, when I had to center everything I was into the precision of my hands. Funny how it still worked, even now, even this way.

I tracked it like a song. A metronome. A prayer.

I wondered if they heard it. The ones who got close. The ones who realized too late that it wasn't just my presence they should've feared—it was the silence inside it. The absence of tremor. The ease.

I exhaled again.

There was a pattern in that too, I think. A rhythm to the way I chose. The way I moved. The way the city pulsed and bent and offered me names I didn't know I needed until I heard them in my sleep. Until I saw their eyes. Until I tasted the edge of their sins.

The breathing was steady.

The silence was whole.

The night was almost ready for what came next.

Was Niko?

His name brushed the edge of my thoughts—not emotion, not longing, just recognition.

The kind a hunter has for the other animal still on its feet.

CHAPTER
THIRTY-FIVE

NIKO

I woke up thinking, stupidly, that today might actually be normal.

Sun through the blinds. Coffee already dripping. Rose in the kitchen pretending not to watch me as I grabbed my badge and holster. A morning like any other before my life turned into this nonstop blur of bodies and shadows and Dante's name carved into the inside of my skull.

I told myself it would stay steady. Controlled. Routine.

I opened the front door.

And everything in me broke.

She was on my porch.

Maya.

Laid out like an offering.

He was here.

Dante had placed her there with careful, deliberate hands and likely stepped back to admire the work.

For a second, just a second, my brain refused to connect the shape to the person. It was the hoodie. Her damn green hoodie she always pulled the sleeves over her palms—always fidgeting with the cuffs when she was nervous, twisting the fabric like it might keep her grounded.

Then I saw what was left of her face.

My stomach went ice cold, then molten, then both at once. The world tipped sideways and didn't right itself.

"No." It came out wrong. Broken. Useless.

I staggered backward, hit the doorframe, and tried to breathe around the wave rising up my throat. Didn't work. I doubled over and vomited into the bushes, my hand shaking so violently it scraped against the brick.

Eyes gone. Ears gone. Tongue...

Jesus Christ.

Her bag was still slung over one shoulder, almost like she'd walked here under her own power. Like she'd knocked. Like I hadn't answered in time.

There was blood everywhere, bright, ugly streaks that looked almost deliberate, like Dante had taken his time dragging his fingers through it.

And then I saw the writing.

Right across the boards of my porch, smeared in thick, wet strokes:

NO SINNER IS SAFE

Everything inside me froze.

The air went dead.

My pulse felt like it turned inward, beating against bone instead of skin.

Maya.

On my porch.

Hours after I'd promised her protection.

Hours after she'd smiled at me and told me she trusted me.

I stumbled forward, dropped to my knees beside her before my brain could stop me. My fingers hovered over her hair, over the sleeve twisted tight in her fist like she'd tried to hold onto something, and I pulled my hand back like I'd been burned.

Her skin had already cooled.

"God... Maya... no, no."

My vision blurred. I didn't even realize I was crying until the tears hit my hands.

I reached for my phone. Couldn't unlock it for three tries. My fingers wouldn't work. My breathing wouldn't either.

The porch, the message, Maya, they all swam in front of me like I was looking through dirty glass.

This wasn't random.

This wasn't about Dante anymore.

This was a message to me.

A threat.

A promise.

The door behind me creaked, and Rose's voice came from inside, drowsy, unaware.

"Niko? Did you forget something?"

I threw my arm back. "DON'T come out here. Rose, stay inside, do you hear me? Close the door, lock it, just do it!"

My voice cracked loud enough to hurt my throat.

She froze.

I heard the lock click.

Good.

Because Maya Sloan, jittery, awkward, sweet Maya who laughed behind her hand and said she was scared of the dark, was dead on my porch.

And he wanted me to find her like this.

He wanted this to be the first thing I saw today.

He wanted me broken.

My hands clenched into fists.

Fine.

He had it. I was broken.

But he was going to pay for it.

And then I heard her.

"Niko...?"

Rose. Behind me. She came out anyway.

I turned, still crouched, shaking like the goddamn world had cracked beneath me.

Her eyes moved from my face to the porch.

To Maya.

To the words.

Her scream wasn't loud.

It was worse than that.

It was quiet. Raw. Like something tearing in her chest that she couldn't put back.

She backed up. One step. Two.

Then, "I can't do this anymore."

Voice hollow.

"I'm fucking done."

"Rose, wait—"

But she was already walking away. Not running. Just leaving.

I stood there, blood on my hands, bile in my mouth, knees in the dirt.

And the woman I loved disappeared down the hall.

Maya was gone.

Rose was gone.

And all I had left was the name burning in my head like a curse:

Dante.

Red and blue lights painted the sky in flashes. Sirens split the air, louder than the scream Rose hadn't let loose.

I didn't move. Couldn't. The porch was slick with Maya's blood, and I stayed there on my knees like the crime scene tape was already coiled around my ribs.

Then came the crunch of gravel. Slamming doors. Voices, muted, then rising.

Caz.

She didn't yell. She didn't joke. She didn't say "Well shit."

She just knelt beside me without touching anything, her voice low and controlled.

"Are you hurt?"

I shook my head.

"Okay. Then get up. You're not helping her by sitting in it."

I let her pull me to my feet. My shirt stuck to my skin, wet and sticky.

DJ came running up behind her, already on the radio calling for backup, for CSU, for someone with more answers than us. He took one look at the message on the porch and stopped cold.

"No fuckin' way..." he whispered. "Is that...?"

Caz raised a hand to quiet him. She was scanning everything, Maya's position, the letters, the direction of the blood spatter. Her face had gone pale, not from fear but from fury held just beneath the surface.

"I was with her last night," she said after a moment, teeth clenched. "She was fine. She was safe."

Medics moved in, trying to navigate around the trail of evidence. A detective from another unit ducked under the crime scene tape being thrown up by patrol, eyes wide. A CSU tech started snapping photos.

I couldn't hear any of it. Just the echo of Rose's voice in my head.

"I can't do this anymore. I'm fucking done."

Caz leaned in again.

"Go sit in the back of DJ's car. Now. Before I have to carry you there."

Her tone didn't invite debate. It wasn't the Caz I knew, the one who made sex jokes at inopportune moments and called me Detective Mopey.

This was the Caz who'd buried friends before. The Caz who could keep her hands from shaking even when her soul was screaming.

"I should've—" I started, but she shut me up with a look.

"No. Not now. You don't get to do that now."

Behind her, DJ walked toward the porch and stared at the blood message.

He didn't crack a joke either.

Didn't even swear.

"'No sinner is safe,'" he muttered, then looked back at us. "We're not just hunting a killer anymore."

Caz exhaled slowly, jaw clenched tight enough to crack.

"No. We're hunting a fucking mission."

CHAPTER
THIRTY-SIX
DANTE

Now why were you outside this house right now, little rabbit?

The street was empty, the sky still heavy with that just-before-dawn hush. She stood on the front step, cute little green hoodie. Just a girl with something gnawing at her chest, maybe a thought she couldn't shake. Maybe a whisper in the dark.

She didn't hear me.

Not until I was already behind her.

I waited, just to see if instinct would kick in, if her spine would stiffen, if her breath would catch, if she'd suddenly remember she wasn't alone. She didn't. She turned like she might go back inside, like whatever ghost she thought she'd seen out here was just her own reflection in the glass.

And I was already stepping through her shadow.

She gasped once, barely a sound really. Not enough to wake anyone. Not enough to matter.

I pressed her against the brick, one hand over her

mouth, the other already slick with steel. I didn't speak. Not at first. She didn't need false comfort. She needed clarity. Purpose.

"You shouldn't be here, Maya."

A whisper, no more than that. My voice pressed into her ear like confession.

"You weren't meant to be part of this. But I figured out your secret."

But the problem with being in the wrong place is that sometimes, it makes you part of it.

The first cut was shallow, intentional. I needed her to feel the moment turn. Her eyes widened, panic blooming behind them. Then the real work began.

Eyes.

Ears.

Tongue.

Fast. Quiet. Efficient.

She shook in my arms, muscles twitching against the pain and the impossibility. Blood pooled in her hoodie. A small, gurgled breath rattled in her throat before she dropped forward onto the porch.

I cradled her there for a second, just a second. Not out of sentiment. Just to feel the silence settle.

In that quiet, I thought of him.

Of the way his face tightens when something slips out of his control. Of how grief doesn't weaken him—It sharpens him. Killing her wouldn't end him. It would wake up him. Strip him raw. Make him dangerous in ways he still didn't understand.

And then I got to work. You know, the usual.

Next, I dipped two fingers in the warmth still leaking from her body and began writing.

One letter at a time across the pale wood of the porch.

N.

O.

S. I. N. N. E. R.

I dragged my hand down, reloaded, and wrote the rest.

I. S.

S. A. F. E.

The blood dried fast in the morning chill, edges darkening as they set. I wiped my hand clean on the hem of her shirt, then gently turned her so her eyes, what remained of them, faced the door. So he would see.

He would wake up, swing that door open like it was any other morning, and he'd know.

She died because of him.

Because he forgot what justice requires.

Because he still hadn't accepted the truth:

No sinner is safe.

Not even him.

Especially not him.

CHAPTER
THIRTY-SEVEN

NIKO

I didn't sleep.

Couldn't, not after what happened.

My front porch still reeked of iron and rot. They'd scrubbed most of it off, but I could still see the faint red outlines if I looked close enough.

NO SINNER IS SAFE

Hard to fucking miss.

Caz and DJ were somewhere in the bullpen arguing over timeline inconsistencies. I was nursing the same cold cup of gas station coffee for three hours. Not because I forgot it, because I didn't care.

I kept going over it.

Over and over again.

Toby. Denise. Calvin. That couple at Fountain Square. Maya.

And then it hit me. Like a goddamn train.

"Wait," I muttered, flipping through the case files. "Wait, wait, wait."

I spread the files out across the whiteboard shelf, hands jittering from caffeine and rage. And there it was.

Denise Hardin: prior DUI with injury, sealed domestic disturbance two years back.

Toby Huntley: assault charge in '97, never served time.

Calvin Ross: former military, dismissed after a brutality allegation that quietly vanished.

The couple in the square: the man was on probation for fraud; the woman had a petty theft charge out of Columbus.

It wasn't just random.

Every single person since the breakout had a rap sheet.

Even Maya—Jesus—she'd told me once, offhand, about getting picked up in college for possession and resisting arrest. Charges dropped. Still.

I stumbled backward and dropped into my chair.

He wasn't just killing anymore.

He was judging.

"Is he some kind of fucking vigilante now?" I said.

DJ looked up. "What?"

"Nothing. Just thinking."

I flipped back further, pre-escape cases.

Frankie Morales: clean.

Eddie Robinson: nothing but a parking ticket.

Casey Renatus: grade school teacher.

Gerald Wolfe: a mechanic. A family man.

The split was clear as day.

Before the prison break? Innocents.

After? Targets.

Caz walked in and stopped mid-sentence when she saw the board. "Oh shit."

"I think I cracked it," I said, pointing to the top left corner. I circled a note in red. Justice is mine.

"That's what he meant," I said, breath catching. "Not that he was claiming the crime. He was claiming the right to decide. Who lives. Who dies."

Her voice was quiet. "Like a purge."

"Like a goddamn reckoning."

She stepped closer. "So... he's judging their sins now? Playing executioner?"

"No," I said, dragging a fresh sheet from the printer tray. "He's not just playing anything anymore. He thinks he's the one who decides. The system failed, so he's making a new one."

DJ raised an eyebrow. "What do we do with that?"

I slammed the marker down and stood.

"We stop pretending this is a manhunt."

Caz tilted her head. "Then what is it?"

I looked at her.

Then at DJ.

Then at the empty chair where Maya was just sitting before she was murdered.

"It's a crusade. And he thinks he's the goddamn messiah."

I wanted to tell Rose. I wanted to hug her and tell her I cracked the case and now we might finally be able to catch Dante for good.

But she was gone.

And it still felt like I was too.

CHAPTER
THIRTY-EIGHT
DANTE

They finally saw it now, at least the edges of it, the outline, the faint silhouette of the truth they'd been too blind or too arrogant or too frightened to acknowledge before, and I could feel their realization like a shift in the wind, a subtle change in air pressure, a soft tremor beneath the city's noise. But it didn't scare me. It didn't slow me. It didn't change the weight of my breath or the rhythm of my pulse, because I always knew they'd get here eventually, that they'd stitch the pieces together and trace the pattern like children connecting dots on a placemat, proud of themselves for discovering a picture that was always already there.

Justice is mine.

I didn't write it as a taunt.

I wrote it as a fact.

A declaration.

A truth older than any badge they polish or oath they cling to.

They want to call it vigilantism, some heated, frenzied spiral of a man who lost control, but they don't understand that control isn't the absence of blood. Control is the decision behind where it spills, and mine had never wavered, not once, not even in the moments when the blade slipped deeper than intended or when the pulse under my fingers fluttered into stillness faster than I meant it to, because the purpose remained pure. Unwavering. Crystalline.

They think it's about sin.

Despite telling them that no sinner is safe, it isn't.

It's about correction.

A world rotting from the inside needs more than laws.

More than trials and cages and half-hearted apologies whispered in front of courtrooms.

It needs consequence carved into the muscle of the city.

And they never understood consequence.

Not like I do.

So I breathed—slow, steady, reverent—while they scrambled and theorized and argued over what it means to kill someone who once hurt someone else, or lied, or stole, or bruised another human being's life with their choices. They argued because they still believed sin had degrees, that suffering had categories, that mercy was a virtue instead of a weakness that allowed rot to spread unchecked.

The girl, Maya, she wasn't meant to be part of it. Not originally. Not in the pattern as it stood. But fate is a sloppy architect, and when I saw her outside that house, when she moved into the dark at the wrong moment, when she became witness instead of bystander, her name wrote itself onto the list whether I wanted it there or not. So I adjusted. I corrected. I made the lines match again.

She wasn't chosen.

She happened.

There's a difference. Turns out she had it coming too, haha. Fate is funny.

But the others?

The others were selected carefully, methodically, with the kind of attention the detectives pretend to possess but never actually wield.

One hurt his family.

One preyed on the weak.

One ruined lives with the flick of a pen and called it business.

One laughed while others bled.

One hid behind religion and thought it made him untouchable.

One thought motherhood erased her cruelty.

One believed that as long as nobody saw the scars, the sins didn't count.

Every one of them carried darkness.

Every one of them walked freely.

Every one of them avoided consequence.

Until me.

And now the detectives stand in some fluorescent-lit room, pointing at the pattern on their board with dry-erase markers and righteous fury, whispering the word vigilante like it's blasphemy, like it's madness, like they can't fathom a world in which someone dares to step into the void they've been too afraid to fill. And I wondered if they even realized how close they were—not just to understanding the truth, but to becoming part of it, woven into the fabric of this judgment they were so desperate to dismantle.

They thought this revelation gave them power.

It didn't.

It gave them clarity. And clarity was a blade sharper than anything I carried.

Because now they knew not just what I did, but why.

And somewhere ahead of me, I saw him—stripped down to what he really was and waiting for the moment we met one last time.

And I could feel her—the woman, the strange one, the one with the sharp eyes and the restless mind—circling the truth with her questions and her jokes and that almost-feral instinct that flickered behind her smile. And she was closer than the others. Closer than she should be. Closer than was safe.

But that's the thing about danger:

Some people smell it.

Some people sense it.

Some people court it.

And some people mistake it for fate.

My breath steadied again.

In through the nose.

Hold.

Out through the mouth.

They were going to tighten their net now, they were going to assign more patrols and heighten surveillance and try to protect the ones they thought might be next. But protection was just another lie they told themselves to sleep better, and lies had no weight in the world I was building. Not anymore.

Justice wasn't delivered by institutions.

It wasn't negotiated.

It wasn't postponed.
It was carved.
It was claimed.
It was carried out.
And I was only getting started.

CHAPTER

THIRTY-NINE

NIKO

Caz leaned back in her chair, boots on the edge of the table like she was about to say something casual. But it wasn't casual. Not this time.

"Prison log from the night of the escape's off by fifteen minutes," she said, tapping her pen twice against the case board. "Guard shift log says 2:03. But the internal system marks it at 1:48."

I blinked. "What?"

"Fifteen minutes. I double-checked it against the CCTV backup timestamps DJ pulled last week." Her voice stayed even. "Doesn't match."

DJ looked up from his laptop. "You sure?"

"I'm sure."

The bullpen went quiet.

I felt the pulse behind my eyes start to throb again, something between a headache and a hangover. The clock on the wall ticked like a metronome made for tension.

237

Caz shrugged. "Could be nothing. But it's worth flagging."

I didn't mean to say it. I didn't even hear myself say it until it was already in the air, slicing everything wide open.

"You could've said that yesterday."

The words froze her face.

I kept going. "You could've brought that up before we lost Maya."

"Jesus," DJ muttered.

"You said the logs checked out. You told me not to obsess over it. You let it go." I took a step forward. "Fifteen minutes, Caz. You know how much can happen in fifteen fucking minutes?"

Her mouth opened, but nothing came out.

"She's dead," I snapped. "And maybe she didn't have to be."

The whole room went still. Even DJ wasn't moving anymore. Just the low hum of the old fluorescent lights and the faint sound of someone typing in another part of the precinct.

Caz dropped her feet from the table and stood. She didn't raise her voice, didn't flinch. She just looked at me, eyes darker than usual.

"You think I don't know that?" she said quietly. "You think I haven't been tearing myself up over every detail since it happened?"

"You sure as hell didn't act like it last night," I fired back.

"Neither did you," she said. "You were too busy giving me shit about the way I look."

I bit the inside of my cheek hard enough to taste blood.

"That's what I thought," she muttered. "Get the fuck outta my face, Russo."

I turned before I could say something worse. Stormed past the desks, out through the hallway, not even registering the people I passed on the way out.

Didn't stop walking until the air outside hit my skin like cold punishment.

I didn't look back.

Because if I did—

I might've seen what I lost this time. And it wasn't just Maya. Not just my fucking father.

It was something breaking loose inside me.

Something I wasn't sure I could glue back together.

And for half a second, I knew I'd just wounded the one person who still understood me—but I kept walking anyway.

***

DJ told me he needed to take me out for a drink.

He didn't talk on the drive.

Not once.

That alone should've tipped me off.

Normally he'd fill the silence with bullshit stories, half-laughs, small talk, or some comment about how exhausted we were. But not tonight. Tonight the quiet felt like a living thing in the SUV, thick enough to breathe in, smoke you couldn't see but sure as hell could taste.

We pulled up to a hole-in-the-wall bar wedged between a vape shop and a payday loan place. The kind of bar where the lights are too dim, the beer's too warm, and the bartenders all look like they stopped giving a shit sometime around the recession. DJ parked but didn't move.

He just sat with his hands still on the steering wheel, thumbs tapping the leather in an uneven rhythm.

"You coming?" I asked.

He sucked in a breath like he was about to dive underwater.

"Yeah," he said. "Yeah. Just... give me a second."

The hairs on the back of my neck rose.

I didn't know why yet.

Inside, the bar smelled like old wood and spilled liquor and the ghosts of every bad decision made in the last thirty years. The floor stuck under my shoes. A neon Bud Light sign flickered like it was on its last warning.

DJ picked a booth in the far corner, away from the regulars, away from the door, away from anyone who could overhear us. He slid in across from me, elbows on the scratched-up table, fingers drumming faster now.

"You want anything?" he asked.

"No."

He nodded like he expected that. He ordered a whiskey for himself. Didn't drink it. Just stared at it.

I waited. Ten seconds. Twenty. Thirty. My patience frayed with each one.

Finally he looked up.

His eyes were red-rimmed. Not from crying—from not sleeping.

"Niko," he started, "there's something I've never told you. Something about... about the night Tony died. But I need you to understand that I miss your dad every single day."

My stomach dropped.

"What are you talking about?" I asked.

He swallowed hard. "I should've said something sooner. I know that." He scrubbed at his face. "I've tried. God knows I've tried. But every time I—fuck—every time I got close, I'd see your face and I'd choke on it."

"What are you getting at?" My voice came out sharper than intended.

He didn't flinch.

"Niko... your dad called me the night he died."

The world went quiet. Not muted—gone.

"What?" I said. "What do you mean?"

DJ nodded, eyes distant. "He called me."

"When?"

"Right before it happened."

I felt something inside me wrench sideways.

"And you didn't pick up?" I asked.

"No," he whispered. "I didn't."

My breath caught. "Why the hell not?"

He closed his eyes. "Because I thought he was spiraling again."

"What?"

"You know how he got," DJ said, voice cracking. "When a case got under his skin too much. When he got that obsessive look. Saying Dante was watching him or calling from blocked numbers or messing with his mail. I—I thought it was one of those nights."

I stared at him. My pulse hammered in my ears.

"I thought he was just scared of his own shadow," DJ said. "I thought he'd call you after. Or text. Or calm down."

My throat went dry.

"But he didn't," DJ said, staring at the table. "And I didn't answer. And by the time the call was over—by the time I even checked my phone—he was already gone."

My voice shook. "What did he say, DJ?"

DJ hesitated. Then lifted his phone with trembling fingers.

"I saved the voicemail," he said.

He tapped the screen. Held it out. Pressed play.

My father's voice—shaken, breathless, terrified—filled the booth.

DJ... I think Dante found me. He's here...

Static swallowed the rest.

I felt the booth tilt. Felt the air thin into nothing. Felt something dark push up from deep inside my ribcage and claw for the surface.

DJ lowered the phone.

"I'm so sorry," he said. "I was wrong. I should've answered. I should've gone to him."

I stared at him because he immediately became someone else—someone smaller, someone weaker, someone who'd held the most important moment of my life in his hand and decided it wasn't worth picking up.

My fingers curled into fists slowly. Quietly. My body was preparing for something my brain hadn't caught up to yet.

"Why the fuck didn't you tell me?"

The question came out hollow.

"I didn't want to throw more weight on you," DJ whispered. "You'd just lost him. And I—fuck, Niko—I was scared of what it would do to you."

I leaned forward, every muscle tight enough to snap.

"You made that fucking decision for me?"

He didn't have an answer.

He didn't need one.

Because the look in his eyes said everything.

And something in me finally—quietly—broke.

CHAPTER
FORTY

NIKO

The door swung shut behind me with a hiss of warm air and cheap neon. DJ followed. I didn't say a word. My hands were already shaking.

He opened his mouth, but I beat him to it.

"You knew."

I wasn't even sure I said it out loud, but it came out somewhere between a whisper and a growl.

DJ nodded once. Cowardly. "I didn't know that, Niko—"

"You knew."

I spun around. He barely had time to take a step back.

My hand hit his chest hard—flat palm, enough to stagger him—but I wasn't done. My knuckles cracked across his jaw, and then again. A flush of heat rushed my face, and I didn't stop to see what landed where. I just needed to hit something.

DJ stumbled against the wall, a smear of blood blooming under his nose. His hands didn't come up to block. He just blinked through it, stunned.

"I needed that call," I said, voice ragged. "He could've been saved. My father could've—"

I stopped. I didn't even know what the hell I was saying anymore. The inside of my skull felt like a firecracker mid-pop.

DJ wiped his nose with the back of his hand. Looked up.

And I don't know what I expected—anger, maybe. A shove back. But he just stared at me, quiet, bleeding, the red catching in the corner of his mouth.

I stepped back. Hands shaking. Chest heaving. I looked down at them—blood and something else. Sweat. Rage. My own heartbeat thudding like a snare drum inside my throat.

I snapped. "You let him die. That's it. That's all that fucking matters."

DJ didn't move. Didn't flinch. He just stared through me like he saw something I didn't.

I hated that look more than the silence.

And just like that—I didn't want to hit him again. I didn't want to look at him again. I turned and walked. Didn't even wait for the sidewalk to split us.

I didn't care if I was being watched. Didn't care if someone saw. Let them. Let the whole city see how far gone I was.

Let *him* see it, too.

I hadn't moved from the floor.

Not since I'd come home to silence.

The house felt hollow. Like a ribcage with no lungs.

I stared at my phone and thought about calling Rose. I didn't. I already knew what the silence would sound like.

But then the phone lit up.

Caz.

> DJ just told me what happened. Where are you? I'm coming over.

> I'm back home. She's fucking gone. I'm sorry for yelling at you. I'm not okay.

I didn't bother cleaning up. I didn't turn on a light. I just sat there with my fists clenched, my jaw tight, my chest a bomb without a timer.

When she got there, she didn't knock. She never knocked. The door creaked open like it already knew it was her, and then she was standing in the entryway like the fuse had just been lit.

Cigarette between her lips.

Black tank.

Jeans riding low on her hips.

Purple hair messy from the wind or from the way she always moved too fast.

And those tits—right fucking there—staring at me like they knew exactly what they were doing.

"You look like shit," she said.

I didn't answer. I was on my feet before I knew it, halfway to her with something boiling behind my eyes.

"I mean it," she said, stepping closer, smoke curling out of her mouth as she flicked the cigarette into the sink. "And your knuckles are red. Niko, did you hit—"

I didn't let her finish.

I grabbed her by the waist and slammed my mouth against hers.

No hesitation. No tenderness. Just raw, breathless need. She gasped against my lips but didn't pull away—she clawed at my back, dragged her nails down hard enough to sting.

Clothes hit the floor like confessions we weren't ready to speak. Her tank top went first, then the bra—black, lacy, practically fucking useless—and her tits were magnificent. Next were her jeans, peeled down those long legs like they were hiding something sacred.

She reached for my belt, yanked it open, shoved my jeans down with enough force to make me stumble back a step. We collided with the wall. She bit my shoulder hard enough to bruise.

"I'm not here to fix you," she growled.

"I'm not asking you to," I snapped.

"Nice cock, Detective," she said, beginning to stroke me. Her hand looked so beautiful wrapped around me, the red string on her finger adding a sensation I couldn't quite name.

I lifted her by the thighs, and she wrapped them around me like she'd been planning this for months. I carried her through the dark hallway to the bedroom—tripped on a shoe, kicked it out of the way, didn't stop moving.

She was already wet when I pushed inside. Tight and hot and desperate. She moaned, loud and unfiltered, head thrown back as I thrust hard, deeper, faster. Her tits bounced just like I imagined they would. Her fingers clawed into my back, hips rolling up to meet every motion.

There was no rhythm. No romance.

Just grief and sex and blood in my mouth from where I'd bitten my own cheek. Her skin tasted like ash and sweat and something I couldn't name.

She flipped us halfway through—straddled me, hair falling around her face, riding me like she wanted control but couldn't quite look away from whatever rage she saw behind my eyes. My hands were on her tits, her ass, her waist—gripping, lifting, pulling her down harder.

She leaned in close, lips brushing mine, breath shaky.

"You fuck like someone who just lost everything."

I looked up at her.

"Then cum for me."

She came with a broken gasp, muscles clenching around me, head tilted back, chest arched. I followed seconds later, spilling inside her with a grunt that felt more like a scream trapped behind my teeth.

But I wasn't done.

I grabbed her hips, still trembling from the aftershock, and flipped her onto her stomach without a word. Her cheek pressed to the sheets, legs parting instinctively as I positioned behind her—hard again, already.

She glanced back over her shoulder, eyes wide but not surprised.

Like she'd expected this. Wanted it. Needed it as badly as I did.

Then she smiled.

I slid back inside her—slow this time.

Deep.

Deliberate.

One hand tangled in her hair, the other gripping her hip hard enough to leave bruises.

She moaned into the pillow, muffled and primal.

"You still think I'm broken?" I growled into her ear, voice torn.

"No," she gasped. "I think you're finally honest."

I didn't answer.

I just kept fucking her until I finished inside her again.

I collapsed beside her, chest heaving, heart pounding like I'd run a mile uphill with a body on my back.

Her skin was damp, flushed, a sheen of sweat catching the early sliver of morning light through the blinds. One leg draped over mine. Her breathing ragged and slow.

For a moment, neither of us moved.

No words.

No lies.

Just the weight of what we'd done pressing down on the mattress like a third presence.

Caz reached for her pack, arms trembling slightly as she fished out another cigarette. Lit it with a flick that felt too casual for what had just happened.

She didn't offer me one. Didn't look at me right away either.

The silence settled thick between us, heavy with the kind of things that never make it out of your mouth.

"You didn't pull away," she finally said, smoke curling from the corner of her lips.

"I didn't want to," I muttered.

"Yeah." She exhaled again. "Me neither."

I turned my head, stared up at the ceiling fan spinning lazy circles like it had all the time in the world to remind me what a mistake this was.

"She's not coming back," I said. "Rose. She meant it."

Caz didn't answer right away.

Then: "I didn't come here to replace her, Niko."

I scoffed. "Didn't say you did."

She stubbed out the cigarette in the candle holder on my nightstand. Let her hand rest there a second too long, then turned back toward me.

"But I'm still here," she said, voice softer now. "And you're still bleeding."

I flinched like she'd touched something raw. Maybe she had.

"I didn't ask for a bandage," I muttered.

"Good," she said. "I wasn't offering one."

We lay like that for a while.

Close. Not touching.

Wreckage cooling between us, the last breath of a fire that shouldn't have started.

Eventually I sat up, ran a hand through my sweat-damp hair.

She looked over at me with a gaze I couldn't quite place —part challenge, part sadness, part something that might've been real if the world were different.

"You really don't see it, do you?" she whispered.

I frowned. "See what?"

But she didn't answer.

And I didn't ask again.

CHAPTER
FORTY-ONE
DANTE

She was circling closer.

I felt it in the shift of her posture, in the questions she let fall like breadcrumbs she hoped I'd trip over. In the way her voice tightened at the edges when she repeated a detail she already knew, just to see if I'd falter. She was smart. She had instincts. She was stubborn and loud and arrogant enough to think she was the one who'd crack it. And maybe she would have—if I hadn't started watching her first.

I saw the moment the suspicion sparked. The way she stood a little straighter by the case board. The way her hand paused too long over the photo of the fountain, her jaw clenched too tight when the blood spelling on the porch was mentioned. Her mind moved like mine. Quick. Pattern-driven. Hungry.

But she was still playing by rules. Still operating under the delusion that law had power over what was already broken.

She didn't know I had been standing ten feet from her when she smiled that morning. Didn't know I had watched the little sway of her hips when she left the station, the smoke curling around her like a halo of rot. Didn't know I had memorized the way her lips moved when she said "fuck."

I knew every angle of her body, every expression she'd ever worn when she thought no one was looking.

And I was always looking.

She was piecing together the aftermath.

But she hadn't seen the design.

She still thought this was retribution. Vengeance.

She didn't understand that this was resurrection.

He understood resurrection better than she ever would. He just didn't know it yet.

She wasn't fast enough.

Not to save herself. Not to save him.

Because the more she dug, the more she thought she was chasing me—

but she didn't know the real rot was already in the room with her.

Breathing beside her.

Sitting in her passenger seat.

Staring back at her in the rearview mirror.

She was going to figure it out.

But not in time.

And when she did?

I would let her scream for him.

And he would come running.

Straight into the dark with her.

FORTY-TWO

NIKO

I didn't move for a while after Caz left. The door clicked shut, and it was like the air just... quit. Stopped circulating. Settled heavy on my shoulders. A weight that didn't come from what had just happened, but everything that led up to it.

I should've stopped myself.

Said something. Anything.

But I just stood there with her lipstick on my skin and her scent in the room and the truth clawing its way up my throat like bile.

Rose was gone. For real this time.

And I let her go.

I pushed her away.

I kept telling myself it wasn't my fault. That Maya's body on the porch, the blood, the message—that would've been enough to destroy any marriage. But deep down I knew I lost Rose long before the blood dried.

I lost her in the hours I didn't come home.

In the way I buried myself in the case, in the anger, in the need to chase something that couldn't be caught.

I lost her when I stopped looking at her like she was real and started seeing her as a reason to keep it together.

I lied to myself about us being okay.

About me being okay.

And now there was nothing left in this house but echoes.

And my guilt.

I wiped my face—still the same me who found Maya on the porch with her eyes wide open and her voice gone forever.

I didn't even realize my hands were shaking until I tried to pour a drink.

It splashed over the counter.

Didn't matter.

I sank into the couch and tried to breathe through it. Just one moment of silence. Of stillness. Something that didn't feel like chaos wrapping around my chest and squeezing.

But then—

Something cut through.

A sharp, rotting stench that didn't belong.

I froze.

At first I thought maybe it was my imagination. The leftovers we never threw out. Something in the trash. The blood still drying on my porch.

But it was stronger than that.

Wetter.

Darker.

It crawled into my nostrils like it had a pulse.

I stood slowly. The bottle sat half-full on the coffee table. I took a breath—and there it was again. Deeper.

Souring the air like death had sunk its teeth into the drywall.

My eyes tracked it.

Down the hall.

Past the coat closet.

Toward the basement door.

The knob was shut.

But the smell was leaking out from beneath it like fog.

Something was wrong down there.

Something was waiting.

I grabbed the flashlight from the drawer.

Not the good one.

Just the shitty plastic one with the batteries I never replaced.

Didn't care.

The stench was worse now.

Like it had found me.

Like it knew I was coming.

The basement steps creaked louder than I remembered.

Each one a crack of bone.

Each one another breath closer to whatever was dying down there.

The air changed by the third step.

Heavier.

Damp.

By the seventh, I had to stop.

Not because I wasn't scared—because I knew I was.

And I needed a second to lie to myself.

For a second, I thought about closing the door. About pretending the smell was just another lie. I could go upstairs. Sit on the couch. Let the house rot quietly around me.

But I kept going.

The flashlight flickered once, twice.

Held steady.

The basement looked the same—tools on the rack, half-finished drywall patch on the far wall, bins of Rose's old school crap.

Nothing moved.

But the smell was thick.

And it wasn't coming from the trash.

It was coming from behind the utility shelf.

I moved it aside.

Slow.

Every joint in the damn thing groaned.

Behind it—a door.

Small. Metal. Old.

Like it had always been there.

Except it hadn't.

Not in my memory.

Not in any of the years I'd lived here.

I reached for the knob.

It was locked.

That stopped me cold.

Because I didn't remember locking this door.

Hell, I didn't remember this door being here at all.

The lock wasn't new.

It was rusted.

Worn.

Tired, like it had been used more than once.

My pulse crawled up my throat.

That smell leaking through the crack beneath it—it wasn't just rot.

It was familiar.

Like something I'd smelled once before and buried so deep I convinced myself I hadn't.

I leaned in.

Pressed my ear to the metal.

Nothing.

I staggered back.

Hit the shelf.

Made it rattle.

A key fell off the shelf right in front of my feet.

Poetic.

CHAPTER
FORTY-THREE

DANTE

The silence beneath the house was patient in a way only time could understand—not the kind of silence that begged to be filled, but the kind that grew fuller the longer it was left alone. The kind that breathed through the cracks and expanded behind walls, stretching into corners no one remembered building.

It was warm that day, which meant the scent spread faster—copper and mold, a memory clotting in the air—and even then, he still didn't recognize it for what it was. He still thought it was a dead mouse, or bad plumbing, or some grief-maddened invention of his own making, because denial was a powerful thing, especially when it was buried under years of guilt disguised as duty.

But he was getting closer.

The steps overhead were heavier now—not just because his body was tired, not just because the floorboards were older, but because every question he'd ever tried not to ask was finally gaining weight. And the house could feel it, the way a wound felt a coming storm.

He was at the basement door now.

It was funny, the things the mind forgot when it wanted to—he didn't remember locking it, didn't remember moving the shelf, didn't remember anything except that low, gnawing pressure in his chest every time he passed it by, like his ribs were trying to hold something in that didn't belong to him.

He paused.

Listened.

It was quiet—not peaceful, but calculated. A quiet that had been watching him longer than he'd been watching himself. A quiet that already knew how this ended.

His hand reached for the knob.

I waited.

The lock held. For now.

But I could feel his breath on the other side—shaky, uneven, not from fear exactly, but from some collision of memory and suspicion and a need to know that outweighed his need to be okay.

There was a time he would've run from this door.

Now he lingered.

Something inside him was shifting—maybe the weight of everything he'd lost, or maybe the slow realization that not everything lost had been stolen.

And there it was—my quiet pleasure of knowing he'd finally arrived where he was always meant to be.

The silence hummed with anticipation.

Because *I was here.*

I had *always* been here.

And soon... so would he.

He would open it.

He would remember.

And when he did, the silence wouldn't need to be patient anymore.

CHAPTER
FORTY-FOUR

NIKO

The key didn't fit.

It should've. I remembered the door now. I'd opened that basement storage door a dozen times before. Old paints, broken lamps, dead cords—nothing back there worth locking. Nothing back there worth remembering.

But this time... the key didn't fit.

It scraped uselessly against the edge of the lock. It was for a different door entirely. One that had no business being in my house.

I crouched, inspecting it. My fingers hovered near the handle like I wasn't sure if I should even touch it.

The lock was new.

Not store-bought either. This thing looked welded on— ugly, industrial, like it had been forced into the wood. The panel around it was splintered and re-stained. Fresh damage layered over old frame. And yet somehow... I hadn't noticed it. I hadn't questioned it. My brain had walked past this door a thousand times and always blinked.

My palms were sweating.

I tried again, firmer this time. Jiggled it. Jammed the key in and turned until the teeth bent and snapped.

Fuck.

I stood up and stepped back, breathing through my nose. Something was humming behind my ribs. That same pull I'd felt outside the precinct. The one I felt right before I found Maya's body.

Like something in the walls wanted me to open this.

It had been waiting.

I grabbed a crowbar from the utility shelf and jammed it between the frame and lock.

Three hits.

Four.

The fifth finally cracked the thing open with a wrenching groan that echoed through the basement like a scream.

I froze.

The door drifted an inch open on its own.

And that's when the smell hit me.

It was the same, sour scent I'd caught on the porch when I saw Maya—before my brain let me understand what it truly meant.

Not just rot.

Something older than rot. Like the breath of something buried alive. Like meat left too long in standing water. Sharp, wet, unnatural. My throat locked up. I covered my mouth with the back of my hand and stepped forward.

The hinges groaned again as I pushed the door open fully.

It was dark inside. No windows. No lightbulb. Just the

hallway glow behind me spilling in and catching a sliver of floor.

The air was still.

And thick.

Each breath dragged like syrup. The humidity stuck to my skin like film. It wasn't a room—it was a fucking tomb.

I reached for my phone and turned on the flashlight.

The beam cut through the dust, now a searchlight.

The floor was unfinished—cracked concrete and streaks of something dark along the edges. The walls were bare cinderblock, sweating. Tarps hung from the ceiling like butcher's curtains. Clear plastic, yellowed with time. And they weren't just draped. They'd been positioned. Intentional. Blocking line of sight.

I stepped forward, slow.

The concrete groaned beneath my boots.

Something sharp crunched underfoot—shards, glass maybe.

And then I saw it.

A dried trail—maroon-brown. Starting near the corner of the room, snaking along the floor. Thick in places. Splattered in others. Like something had bled out here and no one had come to clean it.

Like someone had died down here.

He was here.

In my own home.

I should've backed out. I should've closed the door and called forensics.

But I didn't.

I grabbed my gun and kept moving.

Drawn forward like a fucking puppet.

The trail led behind one of the tarps. One of the larger ones. It bulged at the bottom. Covered something.

My stomach turned.

The light trembled in my hand.

I didn't want to know. But I needed to.

I stepped closer.

Closer.

And the closer I got, the louder the silence became.

No air. No hum of the furnace. No city noise muffled through concrete walls.

Just stillness—thick, pressing, absolute.

I stood over the tarp.

It slumped against the far wall, dragged there. Flies circled above it, slow and content. I crouched—my knees creaked—and reached with one hand.

My fingers brushed the plastic.

Cold.

Not just from the basement chill. From whatever was underneath.

I peeled it back—inch by trembling inch.

First the smell surged up, rich and metallic, gag-inducing. Then I saw the outline. Shoulders. Head. Arms bound tight against the ribs with dried black rope. Clothes long soaked through, skin bloated and graying, mouth slack because it had died screaming.

And the face—

Jesus Christ.

The face was sunken, half-caved on one side. Blood had pooled around the jaw, dried in thick rivulets down his neck. Hair matted and soaked in the back like he'd been lying there for weeks.

No eyes.

No ears.

No tongue.

But I knew him.

I fucking knew him.

"*Dante*," I whispered.

My body wouldn't move.

My knees stayed locked. My heart barely thumped. Every nerve in me stilled—paused in disbelief—trying to catch up to what my eyes were screaming.

Dante Crowe was dead.

Dante Crowe had been in my basement.

Dante Crowe had been in my basement for weeks.

Everything spun. Everything cracked. Every memory of the case twisted and re-threaded itself like a noose.

If Dante was here... then who the fuck—

"No," I breathed. "No, no, no..."

My stomach lurched. I doubled over, nearly retched. My hand gripped the edge of the tarp like it might anchor me to the world.

But it didn't.

Because the world had just shattered.

All the photos. The messages. The murders. The blood on my porch. *No sinner is safe.* The goddamn precision.

It had all been...

Wrong.

Dante wasn't behind this.

He never was.

He couldn't have been.

Because he'd been dead the whole fucking time.

In my house.

CHAPTER
FORTY-FIVE
NIKO

I dropped to my knees.

The second Dante's name crossed my lips, my body revolted. I turned away from the tarp and vomited all over the cracked basement floor. Acid burned my throat, my eyes watered, and the world tilted.

Dante.

Dead.

Here.

This whole time.

I retched again, dry this time, gripping the cement with both hands as if I could keep the truth from swallowing me whole.

My vision blurred.

For a second I thought it was from the smell, the shock, the bile. But then the blur shifted. Colors bled together, walls smeared, and something cold slithered up the back of my skull.

And then—

The flashback hit.

Not a memory.

A rupture.

The prison holding room.

The flickering light.

The chair screeching.

My own breath coming too fast.

Dante laughing.

"You'll never stop thinking about me."

My hands on the table.

My hands curling into fists.

My hands reaching—

No.

No, I didn't—

I let him go. I left—

Except suddenly I wasn't turning away.

Suddenly I was squeezing harder.

The flashback sharpened so violently it made my head snap back. I felt his collar in my fist. Felt his throat under my palm. His pulse hammering once—just once—before my grip tightened even more.

He choked out something—words, maybe—but it didn't matter.

Because I slammed him against the wall.

I felt the impact in my knuckles.

Felt his skull hit concrete.

Felt his breath stutter against my fingers.

And then he slid down the wall.

And I slid down with him.

My hand never letting go until he stopped moving.

I remember waiting for myself to stop.

Waiting for my hands to loosen.

They didn't.

The room was so quiet.

Too quiet.

I heard my own breathing echo. Heard it change. Heard it slow. Heard it turn into something I didn't recognize.

I didn't leave the room.

I never walked out.

The light didn't flicker by accident.

The camera didn't glitch on its own.

Because I was still there.

Kneeling.

Staring at what I'd done.

And then—

The flashback didn't just crack deeper.

It split.

Like someone had taken a crowbar to the hinge of my brain and forced it wide open. The basement vanished, the smell vanished, even the weight of my own body vanished. I wasn't kneeling on concrete anymore—I was kneeling in that holding room.

The exact second after Dante's last breath left his throat.

The world was dim.

Muted.

Silent.

And I was staring at his face.

Slack jaw.

Slack eyes.

Slack everything.

I didn't feel panic. Not yet. Not shock. Not horror.

Just... breathing.

Slow. Controlled. Too steady for what had just happened.

I had my hands braced on my knees like I'd just finished a workout, not murdered a man in a locked room.

Revenge was mine. I killed my father's killer. Justice was served.

Then the flashback lurched forward.

I watched myself reach out, two fingers pressing to Dante's neck.

Checking for a pulse I already knew wasn't there.

Checking like it was routine.

I swallowed hard in the memory—hard now, in the basement—feeling the ghost of that moment tighten around my throat.

My past self looked around the room.

Not as someone caught, but as someone calculating.

The fluorescent light buzzed overhead. It sputtered twice. And I remembered now—I remembered leaning back and tapping the fixture with the end of my baton because it annoyed me.

The same flicker the guards wrote off as a "bad bulb."

I wasn't reacting. I wasn't panicked. I was thinking.

No shaking.

No hesitation.

No remorse.

I crouched beside Dante, grabbed him by the wrists, and pulled him across the floor. His head thumped against the concrete twice—dull, hollow sounds. Sounds I must've heard at the time but remembered as nothing.

My breath hitched. I watched myself drag him to the

corner of the room where the wall met the baseboard—where the camera couldn't fully see.

And right there for me...

A custodial cart.

A mop bucket.

A bundle of folded towels.

A stack of trash bags.

Positioned just so.

Like I had come in knowing exactly how this would go.

I watched myself lift Dante—dead weight, limbs slack—and shove him into the cart. He didn't fit at first. His arm hung over the edge. His knee bent wrong. So I bent it back. Forced it. Jammed him down until the tarp-lined bucket held him.

Then I covered him.

With a towel.

A mop.

A trash bag.

Whatever I could reach.

Like it was a chore, not a corpse.

My stomach twisted. I shook my head hard—trying to pull myself out of the memory—but it kept dragging me back, relentless.

I wheeled the cart out.

The hallway was empty.

The flashback slowed here—like my brain wanted me to savor the detail, the dread.

I pushed the cart toward the staff wing, not the inmate wing.

I knew the layout.

Knew the blind spots.

Knew the off-shift periods.

I'd walked this prison a hundred times during my father's career.

I knew when the night crew swapped.

I knew where cameras overlapped.

I knew how long each guard stayed at their desk.

In the memory, I paused in front of the security monitor room.

And smiled.

Then I entered.

No one was inside.

Shift change.

Just like always.

I shut the door behind me.

The flashback sharpened—the detail too crisp, too brutal.

I watched myself sit at the monitor station.

Watched my fingers move across the keyboard like I'd done this before.

Watched myself pull up the timestamp:

The exact moment Dante died.

Every angle of the room.

Every angle of the hallway.

Every overlapping corridor.

I highlighted them all.

I hit DELETE.

No passcode needed.

No override.

Because I knew the system.

I'd done maintenance for my dad more than once.

Knew the internal back doors.

I wasn't improvising.

I was operating.

Then I rolled the cart to the loading bay.

A guard walked past me.

He nodded.

I nodded back.

He didn't look twice.

And why would he?

I wasn't a suspect.

I was a detective.

I belonged.

The flashback slammed into its final images:

Me loading Dante's body into my trunk.

Closing it.

Locking it.

Driving home with the radio on like it was any other night.

Storing him in the basement and removing his eyes, ears, and tongue.

While laughing.

And when I returned to myself—kneeling in the basement, staring at the real, rotting body—my whole world folded inward.

I hadn't forgotten killing Dante.

I'd buried it.

Something in me had decided it wasn't necessary knowledge.

FORTY-SIX

NIKO

I wrapped the tarp tighter this time. Not like it mattered. He wasn't getting up. But something about it felt necessary. Respectful, maybe. Or cowardly.

My hands moved on autopilot, the tarp rough and stiff with dried blood, its corners creased like a body bag. The smell had stopped bothering me. Or maybe my brain finally gave up trying to translate it—something between rot and rust and every memory I never wanted back.

And then I saw it.

Dante's hand, tucked near the edge of the plastic—just barely peeking out from beneath the folds—had a sliver of red.

Thin. Coiled. Not rope, not wire. A string. On his middle finger. Bright red. So red it didn't belong down here, in this tomb of grey.

My heart stuttered. I knew that string. I'd seen it before.

Caz.

Is she... is she the killer?

I staggered back like it had burned me. Just stared at it. The string. The tarp. The shape beneath it.

I didn't remember putting it there. I didn't remember anything. Except the flashbacks. Except him. Except—

I needed air.

I bolted out the door, climbed into my car, and started driving. Nowhere in mind. Just *away*. Away from the house. Away from the body. Away from the version of myself I couldn't trust anymore.

The roads blurred past. I didn't even know which direction I took. Didn't matter. My pulse was a scream in my ears. My thoughts kept looping.

Red string. Dead man. My hands.

I grabbed my phone.

DJ would answer. He had to.

Dialing...

Voicemail.

> *Hey, it's DJ. You know what to do.*

I hung up before the beep.

Tried again. Nothing. FUCK.

Of course. Just like that night. When Dad needed him most.

DJ didn't answer.

Tires shrieked. Gravel spat from the shoulder as I yanked the wheel back.

I wasn't even trying to die. That was the worst part. I was just... gone. Outside myself. Floating three feet behind my own skull, watching a stranger grip the steering wheel.

My head pounded—not just from the stench I'd left behind, not from the string, not from the silence on DJ's end.

From before.

The crash.

The lights. The chase.

The scream.

The shatter.

The impact didn't hurt the way I'd expected.

It was heat first. Then pressure. Then nothing at all.

That's where this started.

That's where *he* started.

My hands tightened around the wheel. Not from tension. Not from control. From memory.

The neurologist had said there was damage. The doctors had said I was lucky. But I wasn't. I know that now. Something cracked back then. Something inside me that never fused right. It just... split.

One half of me kept showing up to work. Smiling. Kissing my wife. Holding coffee cups and murder boards and Maya's laughter.

The other half crawled into the dark.

And stayed there.

He didn't believe in the system anymore. Not after what Dante did to my father. Not after seeing him sit smug right in front of me. Not after the bullshit sentence. The appeals. The fake remorse. The process.

So that part of me decided to do something about it.

Dante didn't escape. I let the world believe he did.

The truth?

I killed him.

I kept him.

And I kept killing.

Every name on that list. Every victim with blood on their hands.

I called it justice.

But it was guilt.

It was rot.

It was *me*.

I was the one who'd been doing this.

Not Caz. Not DJ. Not the devil who broke my dad.

Me.

And maybe I'd always known it. Maybe that's why I couldn't sleep. Why I kept chasing ghosts I'd already buried. Why I kept accusing shadows when the monster was standing in my own fucking shoes.

I pulled over. Threw open the door.

Collapsed onto the pavement and let the night hold me.

I wasn't sure how long I lay there.

But I didn't cry.

Didn't scream.

I just whispered two words into the dark.

"It's me."

CHAPTER
FORTY-SEVEN

NIKO

I didn't remember driving home.

Didn't remember shutting the door. Kicking off my shoes. Climbing the stairs.

But I was here.

Somewhere between 3 a.m. and whatever the fuck time it was now. Sitting in a dark hallway that smelled like blood and bleach and something else I didn't have the vocabulary for.

My phone was face down on the floor beside me. Buzzing, then silent.

When I picked it up, there were seven missed calls. Three from DJ. Four from Caz.

I didn't remember a single one.

I stared at the screen long enough for the blue light to burn into my corneas. Part of me wondered if I'd even spoken out loud when I said it—when I said "It's me." Or if it had just echoed in my skull, bouncing around the part of me that had finally split open.

A knock came.

Not hard. Not gentle. Just *there*.

And then a voice.

"Niko. It's me."

DJ.

My throat tightened.

"And me," came the second. Caz.

I stayed on the floor for a beat longer. I didn't want to move. Didn't want to open the door and see their faces and pretend I was still whole. Because I wasn't. I didn't know what the fuck I was now—not a cop, not a husband, not even a son worth grieving.

Eventually I made it to my feet.

The door creaked open.

And there they were.

DJ's nose still swollen from the punch. Caz's eyes bloodshot. Her mouth pressed into a line, a cigarette tucked behind her ear like she hadn't slept either.

I couldn't look at them. Not for long.

DJ shifted uncomfortably, like he was about to speak. Caz glanced between us.

I said nothing. Just stepped aside and let them in.

Because the moment I opened that door, everything I'd been running from finally walked inside.

Caz was the first to break the silence.

Of course she was.

"You look like you got hit by a fuckin' hearse."

I didn't respond.

She stepped past me like it was just another night, like I hadn't vanished into the dark and left a trail of wreckage behind me. DJ lingered at the door. He always lingered—that was his thing.

Caz turned in a slow circle, arms crossed, scanning the room.

"So," she said, tone light but probing, "you wanna tell me why DJ called me sounding like a wet paper bag full of panic?"

"I didn't ask him to," I muttered.

"I gathered that." She looked at me. "You okay?"

I didn't answer that either.

DJ cleared his throat. "He called me, then hung up. I came by. He looked... off. I just—I didn't know what to do."

"Okay, first of all," Caz said, "we're not gonna pretend you know what to do in a crisis. You once left a dead possum in your own mailbox for three days because you 'couldn't face the trauma.'"

"That's not fair," DJ mumbled.

"It was *summer*."

Her tone cracked me for a second—I almost smiled. Almost.

Caz walked over to the couch and sat. Not a cop debriefing a witness. A friend. A sharp-tongued, chaotic friend with a badge and more emotional baggage than she could drag behind her.

My eyes settled on the red string on her finger.

She noticed immediately. "What are you looking at?"

"I don't know," I said, barely a whisper.

She started to stand. "Is it—"

"No." I shook my head. "Just... don't."

Something in my voice made her freeze. Her lips parted like she was ready to crack another joke—but she didn't.

Instead, she nodded slowly and sat back down.

Silence again.

The weight of what I couldn't tell them sat heavier than anything I'd ever said aloud.

DJ sat beside her, arms resting on his knees. He looked bruised and exhausted and still bleeding guilt. And for the first time, he didn't look at me like a friend or a partner. He looked at me like someone standing too close to a ledge.

Caz lit the cigarette from behind her ear, took one drag, then remembered she was inside and snuffed it out on her boot. "You ever gonna let us in, Russo?" she asked softly. "We're not just here for shits and giggles. We care."

I looked at her. Then him.

And all I could manage was:

"I'm tired."

Not *I'm sorry*.

Not *I'm fine*.

Just that.

Because it was the only honest thing left in me.

CHAPTER
FORTY-EIGHT
OTHER NIKO

She was going to ask.

She always did.

That needling, nagging hum at the back of the skull—her voice, asking questions she already knew the answers to, dragging light where shadow thrived best.

She poked. Prodded. Pulled.

You okay, Niko?

You've been off lately.

Talk to me.

God, how she talked.

But that wasn't the problem.

The problem was that she *saw.*

She always had.

Saw through the badge, through the pretty partner dance.

Saw through the blood and bleach.

Saw through the man who smiled too long when he wasn't supposed to.

She wouldn't say it yet.

Not out loud.

But it was coming.

I could feel it.

There was a beat before it happened—there always was —where the world got very quiet. Where the birds stopped singing and the engine noise went hollow and the wind didn't rustle the trees quite right.

It wasn't guilt.

It wasn't fear.

It was awareness.

That silence was born the night metal screamed and everything went black for a half second too long—and when he came back, I was born.

The machine inside began to calculate:

What does she know?

How did she find it?

What's her next move?

Because I couldn't have her take this away from me.

This balance.

This clarity.

It had never been about rage. Never about chaos. It had been about *right*. About the kind of justice the courts couldn't promise and the system never delivered. I held it in my hands. I gave it shape. I gave it blood. I made peace by making war.

She wouldn't understand that.

She'd try.

She'd look at me with those pitying eyes, like she was still holding out hope for the version of me she first met.

But he wasn't here anymore.

He got buried with my father.

She was going to ask.

She always did.

And when she did...

Well.

That's when I'd know what kind of ending this story deserved.

It was different now.

There was no name to hide behind. No mask to blame. No Dante to hunt.

There was only *me*.

I'd tried to split it—to make space between the hands that held the scalpel and the hands that held the badge. But they were the same hands, weren't they?

Same nerves. Same fingerprints. Same knuckles that cracked when DJ hit the ground.

And she saw that.

The way she looked at me after—it wasn't fear. Wasn't pity.

It was *recognition*.

The kind that wrapped around your throat slow and quiet, like a noose made of memory.

She was going to ask.

She always did.

But this time, she wouldn't stop at questions.

This time she'd push.

And I didn't know what I would do if she didn't stop pushing.

Maybe I'd beg her to leave.

Maybe I'd lie again—a better one this time, a cleaner fracture.

Or maybe I'd finally admit it.

That I was there.

That I never left that cell.

That the first time I killed, it wasn't rage or revenge or trauma—it was *relief*.

That when Dante's body went still, something inside me went still too.

Like the volume of the whole goddamn world turned down and I could finally think again.

She was going to ask.

She always did.

And when she did...

I didn't know which one of us would survive it.

CHAPTER

FORTY-NINE

NIKO

DJ and Caz didn't stay long.

They hovered in the doorway for a minute—DJ with that disappointed-dad slump, Caz with a half-sarcastic quip that didn't quite land. And then they were gone. I watched their taillights pull away, twin red dots sinking into the dark—a warning I wouldn't let myself read.

The house felt wrong without them.

Too quiet.

Too aware.

I was still standing in the living room, trying to decide if I should sit or pace or crawl out of my own skin, when the front door opened again.

I thought it was Caz at first. Coming back for round two. Another joke to cut the tension. Another look that told me she'd been clocking every crack in my armor.

But it wasn't Caz.

It was Rose.

She stepped inside, clearly not sure she was even allowed to anymore. Her keys hung limp in her hand. Her eyes were swollen, cheeks blotched red—like she'd cried in the car for a long time before working up the courage to come in.

"Hey," I said, my voice catching halfway out of my throat. "Rose—"

"Don't," she said.

Just that one word. Soft. Final.

She shut the door behind her and leaned against it, arms crossed tight over her chest. She didn't take off her coat. Didn't move any closer.

Something dropped in my stomach—heavy as stone.

She let out a shaky breath.

"I didn't come here to fight."

My mouth opened—for what, I didn't know. An apology? A promise? A lie? None of them found their way out.

She looked at me—really looked—and her expression wasn't anger. It was sadness. Exhaustion. The kind of hurt that doesn't leave bruises but leaves scars.

For a second, I remembered the way she used to look at me when she thought I was asleep.

"I can't do this anymore, Niko."

The words hit harder than the crash. Harder than the truth in the basement. Harder than the flashbacks tearing open my skull.

"I want a divorce."

I didn't breathe. Couldn't. My chest locked up, ribs cinching tight like someone was pulling a belt around them.

"Rose, please—"

"It's not a decision I made tonight. Or yesterday. Or last week." Her voice trembled, but she held her ground. "I've been losing you for a long time. Piece by piece. And I kept hoping you'd come back. I kept waiting for some part of you to realize how far you've gone."

"I'm trying—"

"You're obsessed," she said. "You're drowning in it. And you don't even see the people reaching for you anymore."

Her eyes glistened. "You don't see me."

I swallowed hard, but the lump in my throat didn't move.

She shook her head, looking down, maybe ashamed of her own words. "I didn't want it to end this way. I didn't want to walk away from you. I just..."

She blinked fast. "I can't watch you destroy yourself anymore."

I opened my mouth to beg, or argue, or collapse, but then her eyes drifted.

To my neck.

Her expression froze.

Her lips parted, but no sound came out.

And before she even spoke, I knew.

Because I felt it—the weight of what I hadn't cleaned, hadn't seen, hadn't cared enough to hide.

Her voice cracked like glass:

"Niko... what is that on your collar?"

My heart stopped.

I looked down.

A smear of dried, rust-colored blood.

Not mine.

Dante's.

I froze.

Not because of what she said. But because I could feel *him*—

Stirring.

Gnawing.

Rising.

Rose stood motionless in the doorway, eyes locked on my collar. I followed her gaze like a slow-motion reel I couldn't rewind, couldn't pause. Just the edge of it. A blotch of red, rusted and smeared. A dried scream.

"Is that—" she began, but I couldn't hear the rest over the pounding of my pulse.

My mouth opened. Nothing came out.

She stepped back. "What the fuck, Niko."

I reached for her. I don't even know why. Maybe to explain. Maybe to stop her.

Maybe because the thing in my chest wasn't guilt.

It was hunger.

But she flinched like I was the monster in her night-mares and not the man who used to hold her in the dark, whispering promises we both knew I'd break.

"I should've left a long time ago," she said, her voice cracking but still sharp enough to gut me.

Inside me, something clicked.

Not loudly. Not violently.

Just... clicked.

Like a drawer closing.

Like a lock turning.

I blinked again and looked down. My hands were trembling. Not from rage. Not from panic.

From restraint.

He was closer now. I could feel him. Peering through the cracks. Pressing against the seams of who I thought I was.

And all I could think—

The only thing that made sense anymore—

Was that she saw it before I did.

That she always had.

CHAPTER
FIFTY

NIKO

I opened my mouth to speak.

To say something—anything—that might unfreeze her face, smooth the tension in her shoulders, explain away the blood, the silence, the stench clinging to my skin. I opened my mouth—

But it wasn't my voice that came out.

It was too even.

Too clean.

Too cold.

Rose blinked. So did I.

She tilted her head, confused. "What did you say?"

I hadn't said anything.

Or maybe I had. Maybe that was the problem.

My tongue felt too big in my mouth, like it didn't fit anymore. My jaw twitched, like it had a mind of its own. I took a step back and swallowed hard, trying to reset something—reset *me*—but the glitch was still there, buried somewhere deep in my throat.

Rose crossed her arms. "Niko, what the hell is going on with you?"

I didn't answer. I was listening. Not to her—but to myself. To the echoes in my skull. Something was off, wrong, misaligned.

My chest rose and fell like I'd just run a marathon, but my hands were still. Too still.

"I think I need to lie down," I mumbled. But even that sounded... warped.

Rose frowned. "You okay?"

I nodded.

Lied.

She stepped closer. "You're scaring me."

I looked at her and felt everything all at once—love, guilt, shame, the weight of the basement pressing up through the floors—and none of it moved my face. None of it cracked through the surface. Because something else was swimming beneath it.

Watching.

Waiting.

I turned away before I could scare her more.

But in the hallway mirror, just before I vanished from view, I caught it.

A flicker.

A smile.

Not mine.

I stood in the kitchen, hands on the sink, trying to remember what breathing was supposed to feel like.

Behind me, I heard her move. Softly. Cautiously. Almost as if she knew she was approaching a wounded animal that might still bite.

"Niko," she said. Quiet. Unsure. "Say something."

I turned.

Her mouth was open—but her eyes were closed. Not fully, just squinting, like she was trying to convince herself she wasn't seeing what she was seeing.

"I'm fine," I told her.

My voice—*my voice*—came out smooth, even, neutral. Like I'd been practicing it. Like I'd said it a hundred times already today.

Her jaw tensed. "No. You're not."

I tried to step toward her.

She stepped back.

It landed like a knife in the base of my spine.

Rose searched my face, her breath catching. "There's something wrong with you."

She said it like she was only just realizing it wasn't new.

Like maybe it never went away after the accident.

Like maybe it started *because* of it.

"I didn't notice it at first," she said, scanning me like a stranger. "But it's been there for a while. The way you talk sometimes. The blank spots in conversations. How you... drift."

Her hand lifted slightly. It shook. She didn't seem to notice.

"After the accident... after the coma... there were moments. I thought it was just trauma. The grief. The stress. But this..." She swallowed. "This is different."

I didn't speak.

I couldn't.

Because she wasn't wrong.

Because I remembered too.

The pressure behind my skull when I woke up in that hospital bed.

The way time fractured when I looked at my father's body. When I stood over Dante's.

The silence that took root inside me.

She took another step back.

And then she whispered the only thing I wasn't ready to hear:

"You didn't survive that crash, Niko. Not all of you."

Something ignited.

Not in the air.

Not in the room.

In me.

I blinked, and I was standing closer.

Too close.

"I remember the man who used to hold my face in both hands when he was overwhelmed," she whispered. "And you're not him right now."

"I can explain," I said.

But my voice was too fast.

Too calm.

It didn't sound like me—and I knew it.

Worse: she knew it.

Rose was backed against the far side of the kitchen island now, her fingers curled white-knuckled around the edge, the only thing tethering her to reality. Her breath came shallow, frantic. And her eyes... God, her eyes—they weren't just scared.

They were *searching*.

For me.

"Niko, what's happening to you?" she whispered.

"I don't know."

That part was true.

"Then tell me what you *do* know. Right now."

I opened my mouth. Closed it. Opened it again.

"I found him," I said. "I found Dante."

Her eyes widened. "What?"

"In the basement."

She flinched. Like I'd just dropped a bomb between us. Her gaze darted toward the hallway. Toward the stairs. Back to me.

"You... you found him? You mean—he's—he's dead?"

I nodded.

"I don't understand—how did he get in there? Why didn't you call the police?" Her voice cracked. "Niko, that man ruined your life. You've been chasing him for years."

I stepped forward slowly, hands raised.

"I did."

The words came out low. Heavy. "I caught him. A long time ago. And I killed him."

She didn't move.

Didn't blink.

Just stood there shaking as the weight of it pressed into her chest.

"But that was before," I said, choking on each syllable. "Before all this. Before the others. I thought it ended with him. I thought I could breathe again. But then..."

I looked down. My palms. My shoes. The dried blood I hadn't seen before.

"Then the bodies started showing up. And I thought— fuck, I thought it had to be Dante. That maybe we'd missed something."

Rose covered her mouth. "But it wasn't Dante."

My throat burned.

"No."

She took a step forward. "You've been blacking out. Haven't you?"

"...yes."

"And you don't remember the kills?"

"No. Not all of them."

She exhaled hard, eyes filling. "Jesus, Niko. This whole time... I thought you were chasing a monster. I didn't know *you* were the fucking monster."

I shook my head violently. "No. No, I'm not. Not all of me."

"Then what is it?" she snapped, tears streaking down. "What the hell is driving you when you're not you?"

And I didn't have an answer.

I wanted to say it was trauma.

Or grief.

Or rage.

Or some fluke in the brain that splintered on impact.

I wanted to tell her the truth—that I wasn't content with the type of justice my father got.

But all I said was:

"I don't know how to stop it."

She stepped toward me.

"Rose... don't."

My voice cracked in the middle, something snapping inside it. My hands lifted instinctively, palms out, a warning. A plea.

She froze for half a second.

Then she moved anyway.

"No," she whispered, shaking her head, tears streaking. "I'm not leaving you like this. I'm not walking away while you're—"

"Don't come closer."

It came out sharper this time—a cut through the air.

Her breath hitched, but she didn't stop.

She never stopped when she loved something broken.

"You need help," she said, stepping around the island. "Real help. We can get you a doctor. We can go to the hospital. They have specialists for—"

"Rose."

My voice dropped.

"Stop."

She didn't.

Another step.

Another breath.

Another inch into danger she didn't understand.

"Baby, look at me," she said softly. "Please. Just look—"

I did.

And that was the mistake.

Because the second our eyes met, I felt him surge—the thing coiled behind my ribs, the presence that wasn't entirely mine, the cold clarity crawling up my spine. A parasite learning to stand.

Her face blurred.

Her voice warped.

The room tilted.

I backed up so fast I nearly tripped.

"Rose—stop." My voice broke open. "Please. You have to run."

She froze.

For the first time, she listened.

I collapsed.

My knees hit the tile hard—a crack of bone against floor that vibrated up my spine and stole the breath from my lungs. My palms slapped down next, then my forehead. I curled in on myself, sobbing into the cold linoleum—a man begging a storm not to drown him.

"Please go," I whispered, choking on the words. "You don't understand—he's—he's not— I can't—"

She stared at me.

Hands trembling.

Heart breaking so loudly I could almost hear it.

"Niko," she breathed, voice cracking, "you're scaring me."

"I should," I sobbed. "I should scare you. Get out. Please, Rose, just run."

My whole body shook.

My fingers clawed weakly at the floor trying to hold on to the man I used to be.

But he was slipping.

He'd been slipping for a long time.

And Rose finally saw it.

All of it.

She didn't scream.

She didn't bolt.

She just stood there—torn between love and terror— watching the man she married unravel on the kitchen floor.

CHAPTER
FIFTY-ONE

OTHER NIKO

Well, Rose was too close now.

Too close to the truth, too close to the fracture line, too close to the place where I ended and he began. There had been a time—

a softer time, a quieter time—

when she could stand in the doorway, whisper my name, touch my face, and I would come back.

But that time was gone. It had dissolved the night the skull cracked and the world split cleanly down the center.

She didn't see that yet.

She still thought she was talking to him.

She thought her voice could hold him together, that her hands—trembling as they reached for me—could pull him back into one solid shape.

But there was no shape anymore.

There was only the fracture.

The wound.

The echo that had grown into something with teeth.

She stood there now, tears striping her face, whispering pleas she didn't understand, begging a part of him that wasn't here and would never be here again. Her heart was loud. So loud. Loud enough to drown out reason. Loud enough to mask danger. Loud enough to make her believe she could save him.

But she couldn't.

She was too close now.

If she left this house, the world would follow her back.

The cops.

The questions.

The forensics.

The suspicion.

All the threads we had tied, all the justice we had carved, all the lies we buried beneath floorboards and tarps and time—they would unravel the second she opened her mouth.

She hadn't committed a crime.

No sin.

No blood on her hands.

And still, some part of me respected her for staying when every instinct was probably telling her to run.

But innocence didn't matter here.

Not when the stakes were this high.

Not when the truth was this sharp.

Not when she stood on the brink of becoming the one loose thread in a tapestry woven with bone.

We couldn't let her leave.

Not because she deserved punishment.

No.

Not her.

But because she could undo everything.

And we had come too far.

Balanced the scales too carefully.

Held the world in place with too much precision to let one trembling woman collapse it with a single breath.

She loved him enough to stand in the dark with him. That was her mistake.

She didn't know it yet.

She didn't know that the man she loved was kneeling on the kitchen floor while something else stood behind her—quiet as a shadow, patient as the grave.

But she was about to.

Because she was too close now.

Maybe this closeness was a kind of sin.

One that we couldn't allow to go unanswered.

CHAPTER
FIFTY-TWO

NIKO

She didn't move.

Not at first.

She just stood there in the doorway, arms shaking at her sides, mouth parting as if she wanted to scream but no sound came out. Her eyes were fixed on me—no, not me. On the thing inside me. On whatever the hell had just taken control of my voice.

I couldn't feel my legs.

My lungs seized.

Her gaze darted from the blood on my collar to the jagged tear down my sleeve. To my knuckles—still red. She stepped closer, just one foot forward, and I recoiled like she was holding a match to gasoline.

"Don't come closer," I rasped. "Please—don't."

She ignored me. Tears flooded her eyes now—not out of fear, but heartbreak.

"You've been different since the crash. Since your dad…"

Her voice shook. "I didn't want to believe it. I thought it was grief, or stress—Jesus, Niko, I thought maybe you were having a breakdown. But this—"

She gestured wildly. "This is something else. You black out. You say things like you're someone else. And now—"

Her hand covered her mouth.

"I've seen this before," she whispered. "In patients. TBIs that fracture memory. Split personalities, they used to call it. Like your brain can't hold the trauma anymore, so it... divides."

I was sobbing now. Not soft tears—ugly, wet, gut-splitting sobs that collapsed my whole chest. I staggered back until I hit the wall and slid down like a crumpled rag.

"I didn't want this," I whispered. "I didn't want any of this."

"I tried to forget." My nails dug into my scalp. "I thought he got out. I really thought Dante escaped."

A pause.

A tremble in her lip.

I reached out a trembling hand. "Please... run."

But she didn't.

She knelt. She stayed. Even now.

And I felt it again—something rising in my chest that didn't belong to me.

That was when the voice came back.

Inside my head.

Cold.

Steady.

She's too close now. We can't let her leave. Even though she didn't commit a crime, we can't be caught.

And I screamed—

A blood-curdling, desperate scream—

"RUN, ROSE!"

I didn't feel myself stand.

I didn't feel my feet move.

I only felt the drop—

that sickening internal fall when the other presence snapped into place like a second spine.

Rose's eyes widened.

She knew.

She finally knew.

"Ni—Niko, wait—"

I lunged.

Not toward her.

At her.

My hands crashed into her arms, shoving her backward into the hallway wall so hard the picture frames rattled and tilted. She gasped, pain flashing across her face, but she still refused to scream.

"STOP!" I yelled—or I thought I yelled—but the sound that left me was wrong. Too deep. Too sharp. Too steady.

She pushed back, palms against my chest. "Niko, listen to me—fighting me won't fix this—you're hurt—your mind is—"

But the pressure in my skull was volcanic, molten—a roar louder than her voice, louder than anything in the house.

She's trying to expose us.

We can't let that happen.

We finish what was started.

"NO!"

I slammed my forehead against the doorframe to drown the voice out. The crack of bone on wood rang like a gunshot. Blood trickled into my eyebrow.

Rose screamed.

Not in fear—

in grief.

She grabbed my face, forcing me to look at her.

"Fight it! Fight it! Niko, please—please come back—"

I remembered the way she used to squeeze my hand twice when she was scared, like a secret signal that meant *stay*.

For a second—just a second—her voice reached me.

Her face, blurred with tears, pulled me forward out of the fog.

"I—I'm here," I whispered. "Rose, I'm here—"

But the second broke.

A white-hot spike seared through the center of my skull, and my vision went dark at the edges. The killer—the thing inside me—surged like a second heartbeat.

My hands clamped around her wrists. Too hard.

She cried out, trying to pull away, but I dragged her back.

We crashed to the floor together.

Her elbow hit the tile with a sickening crack.

She screamed—high, raw, terrified.

My chest heaved.

My breath came in animal bursts.

I tasted blood.

I didn't know whose.

"Niko—stop—Niko, STOP—"

I felt my hands shift from her wrists to her shoulders.

Pinning her.

Holding her down.

No—

He was holding her down.

"PLEASE!" she sobbed. "THIS ISN'T YOU!"

Her words hit like a blow.

My grip loosened… barely… but enough for her to pull one hand free and press it to my cheek, cupping my face with trembling fingers.

"I love you," she whispered. "Come back to me."

For one final, impossible heartbeat—

I did.

And then—

Everything went red.

Her scream split the air.

My body moved.

Her nails raked across my arm.

Something warm splashed my shirt.

Something broke.

Something stopped.

Then—

Silence.

A ringing silence so deep it felt like drowning.

I looked down.

My hands were shaking.

Blood streaked my fingers.

Her body lay still beneath me.

"Rose?"

My voice broke.

"Rose? ROSE—"

Nothing.

Just the sound of my own breath collapsing into itself.
And then, from somewhere deep inside—
somewhere cold, triumphant, inevitable—
It had to be done.
We can't be caught now.
We finish this alone.

CHAPTER
FIFTY-THREE

NIKO

My hands wouldn't stop shaking.

I tried to lift her, straighten her—do something, anything—but she was limp, sliding through my grip like she was made of water.

"Baby, come on, come on—look at me—please—"

Her eyes were half-open.

Unfocused.

Still.

No.

No, no, no.

I pressed my ear to her mouth. Nothing.

No breath.

No flutter of warmth.

A sound tore out of me—something animal and broken—and I locked my hands over her sternum and started compressions.

"One—two—three—four—"

My palms slipped. There was blood under them. I didn't even know whose.

"FIVE—SIX—SEVEN—COME ON, ROSE—BREATHE—"

My arms burned. My chest burned.

The world blurred at the edges as I leaned down and breathed into her mouth.

Her lips were cold.

Too cold.

"Please—please—"

I went back to compressions, harder this time, her chest popping under the pressure.

"COME BACK—DON'T—DON'T LEAVE ME—DON'T—"

Tears blinded me.

They fell onto her cheeks like she was crying too.

Another breath.

Another.

Another.

Nothing.

"ROSE!"

My voice cracked, my throat ripping raw.

I tried again—harder, faster—trying to force her heart to remember how to beat.

It didn't.

It wouldn't.

"Please…"

My voice was gone.

Just air. Pain. Begging.

"Please, baby—please—don't do this—don't—don't go—"

My palms shook too much to keep the rhythm. I pressed

my forehead to hers, still doing compressions with one hand, sloppy and hopeless.

"Rose... I'm sorry... I'm so fucking sorry..."

Nothing.

Not a twitch.

Not a breath.

Not a heartbeat I can pretend I felt.

The truth settled in slow, horrific inches—

She was gone.

And I was the reason.

I folded over her, clutching her shoulders, rocking like I could will life back into her body.

"I didn't mean it... I didn't mean it... come back..."

But the house was silent.

And she didn't move.

The refrigerator hummed, steady and oblivious, like nothing had changed.

I didn't remember moving. Didn't remember the sound that tore from my throat, or the wet heat still on my hands. All I knew was that I was suddenly in the far corner of the room, my back pressed so hard against the wall it might've cracked.

Everything was still.

Too still.

The whole house felt vacuum-sealed, the world outside no longer real. The only sound was my breathing—shallow, uneven, too fast. Then slower. Then nothing. Just silence.

I stared at her.

No. Not her. Not like that.

My brain refused to stitch the image into something real. It splintered instead—scattered like blood across drywall, like memories that couldn't be mine. This wasn't supposed to happen. Not like this. Not to her.

My hands wouldn't stop shaking. My fingers twitched like they were still trying to undo what they'd done. Blood pooled on the floor—hers, mine, maybe both. I couldn't tell anymore. I didn't want to.

A low sound leaked out of me. Not a sob. Not really. More like something broken trying to remember how to be whole.

I curled tighter, knees to my chest, pressing my forehead against them like I could disappear—shrink myself small enough to hide in the cracks between floorboards. Maybe if I got small enough, I could rewind time. Undo the door. Undo the basement. Undo everything.

She had just been trying to understand.

And I told her to run.

I begged her to run.

But I didn't stop.

The room pulsed with memory—ghost echoes of her voice, her breath, the last look in her eyes. My mind replayed it on loop, frame by frame, until I wasn't sure what I'd seen and what I'd imagined.

Then came silence.

The kind of silence that swallowed everything and left nothing behind.

CHAPTER
FIFTY-FOUR
OTHER NIKO

The gun felt heavier tonight. It had grown a spine, a pulse, a mind of its own. I turned it over in my hands slowly, letting the metal catch the low light of the room—a dull gray shimmer, nothing bright, nothing alive. It had never been meant for her. It had never been meant for anyone except him. Except me. Except us.

A tool.

A tether.

A last resort.

I slid my thumb across the chamber. Warm. It shouldn't have been warm.

Metal shouldn't hold heat like that, but somehow it did —like it remembered the shape of his palm, the sweat, the tremor. He thought this was the only way out. The clean way. The easy way. The way that left no loose ends for the world to tug.

But I didn't want clean.

I didn't want easy.

I wanted control.

The first bullet slipped out of the cylinder with a soft clink, rolling across the floorboards until it found a crack and nestled inside it. I watched it disappear. Swallowed whole. Gone. One less option for him. One less voice that might talk him into doing something reckless, something final, something cowardly.

I released another.

And another.

Slow, deliberate movements—almost tender.

Like peeling petals from a dying flower.

They piled around my feet, tiny brass bones, each one holding a future that would never happen now. A future he thought he deserved. A future I could not let him choose.

The gun grew lighter, piece by piece, breath by breath, until it felt almost hollow.

Like me.

I held it up, sighting down the empty barrel into nothing. The room swam at the edges. My breathing evened. The quiet settled. Even the blood on the walls seemed to fade under the weight of that stillness.

He was curled up somewhere behind the eyes—shaking, pleading, whispering apologies that came far too late. I felt our mouth move. I felt his effort. But whatever came out wasn't a voice—just breath scraping past teeth. Nice try. I could feel him pressing against the inside of our skull like someone pounding on a locked door.

Please stop, he said.

Like I was the problem.

Like he wasn't the reason any of this began.

He shouldn't have looked.

Shouldn't have dug.

Shouldn't have chased the truth into the dark and expected it not to look back.

He brought us here.

He built this cage, sealed its doors, buried the evidence, wove the lies into his own memory until he didn't know where he ended and I began.

He made me.

And now he wanted me to stop.

My hand opened. The gun dropped to the floor. Empty. Useless. Harmless.

A final bullet rolled against my toe. I nudged it away.

He was sobbing now—somewhere deep in the marrow of us—drowning, collapsing inward, desperately clawing for control he had never actually held.

And I listened.

For once, I listened.

The house was still.

The night was still.

The world was still.

And I offered him the only mercy he had earned.

A whisper—soft enough that only the inside of our skull could hear it:

"You asked me to stop. And so I did."

FIFTY-FIVE

NIKO

I didn't remember getting off the floor.

I didn't remember washing my hands.

I didn't remember picking up the pen.

But I was sitting at the kitchen table, Rose's blood drying in patterns across my shirt, and my hand was moving without me—scratching, dragging ink across paper that kept blurring in front of me.

The note started itself:

> DJ—
>
> I'm sorry. You were right. You tried.
> I should've seen it. I should've listened.
>
> Caz—
>
> I didn't mean for you to get close.
> I didn't mean for you to see any of this.
> You didn't deserve to be pulled in.

The letters twisted, shook, smeared. My fingers wouldn't hold steady. My breath kept breaking. I couldn't tell which parts were me and which parts were... not.

I wanted to tell them everything.

I wanted to explain the basement.

The body.

But there weren't enough words.

There wasn't enough space.

So I wrote the only thing I knew for sure:

> *I didn't want to hurt her.*
> *Please believe that.*

I stared at the page.

I didn't recognize my handwriting anymore.

My chest caved inward.

The house felt wrong.

Too quiet.

Too full.

I pushed the chair back. It screeched across the floor, the sound sharp enough to make me flinch.

And then—

BANG. BANG. BANG.

My name—screamed, panicked, furious—from the other side of the front door.

"NIKO! OPEN THE DOOR! NOW!"

DJ.

Then another voice—sharper, breathless:

"Russo! You open this fucking door or I will shoot the lock off myself!"

Caz.

The pounding intensified. The doorframe rattled. They must've heard Rose scream. They must've come running.

Of course they had.

Because they still believed there was something left to save in here.

I closed my eyes and grabbed my gun.

The metal felt colder now.

Honest.

Like it knew exactly what it was meant to do.

I pressed it to my temple.

For the first time all night, everything inside me went still.

I pulled the trigger—

Ready for it all to end—

and nothing.

For half a second, I was nothing but terror—trapped in my own skull.

Are you fucking serious?

I'm not letting you kill us.

This is just who we are now.

The door didn't just open—

it *exploded.*

A crack—splinter—then the entire frame gave under DJ's weight.

Caz was behind him, gun raised, hair wild, chest heaving.

For a second they stood frozen in the doorway—two silhouettes staring into hell.

Then they saw.

Rose.

The blood.

Me on the floor with a gun to my head.

DJ's face drained. His mouth opened, but no sound came out.

Caz stumbled backward like someone had punched the breath out of her.

"Niko—" DJ finally choked, voice splitting. "What the hell did you—what happened—what did you do?"

I looked up at them.

Or maybe we did.

Because something slid forward inside my skull—

a shadow stepping into the light.

My hand dropped from my head.

The gun clattered to the tile.

And when I spoke—

...it wasn't me.

It was smoother.

Lower.

Too calm for this room.

"Niko asked me to stop."

DJ's eyes widened.

Caz raised her gun higher.

"Niko," she whispered, "I swear to God—don't—"

The voice ignored her completely.

"So I did."

DJ shook his head slowly.

"No. No, no, no—stop. Stop talking like that. Just stop."

Caz stepped forward, gun aimed dead at my chest, her eyes locked on mine like she was staring down a rabid thing.

"I didn't stop killing Rose," the voice said.

"I stopped being Niko."

Caz's breath vanished.

DJ's lips trembled.

Neither of them looked like they were seeing a friend anymore.

They were seeing the truth.

The thing wearing my skin *smiled*—my lips pulling into a shape I didn't recognize.

"He *was* here."

A pause.

A slow blink.

A tilt of the head that had never been mine.

"Not anymore."

DJ staggered back, hand over his face, horror stretching his features.

Caz didn't move.

Not forward.

Not back.

She only whispered, like her body forgot how to breathe:

"...Holy shit."

Inside me—far, far away—something clawed at the walls, screaming, begging them to run.

But the monster drove the body now.

And he was finished hiding.

FIFTY-SIX

NIKO

DJ moved first.

A raw, broken sound tore out of him—half-rage, half-grief—and he lunged straight at me with both hands.

For one suspended heartbeat, I saw every memory flashing behind his eyes:

Me and him in training.

Me sitting beside him when his mom died.

Me holding him after Tony's funeral.

And then—

Impact.

His shoulder slammed into my chest and we crashed backward into the counter. Pain spiked up my spine, but something inside me laughed. *Actually laughed.*

The sound spilled out of my throat—wrong, sharp, delighted.

"DJ," I heard myself say, "you should've answered the phone."

DJ roared and swung.

His fist connected with my jaw so hard my vision exploded white. My head snapped sideways. Blood filled my mouth.

Good, I thought—or maybe *he* did.

Someone inside me thought that was good.

But the body didn't go down.

My hand snapped up, grabbed DJ's shirt, and yanked him forward, slamming him into the floor. His skull cracked against the tile and he groaned.

"GET OFF HIM!" Caz screamed.

Then she was on me.

Caz hit like she'd been waiting her whole life for permission.

Her forearm hooked across my throat, legs braced, body weight driving down. She tried to pin my shoulders, but I bucked hard and she nearly lost her grip.

"NIKO!" she shouted. "Niko, listen to me—LISTEN!"

Her voice trembled.

Not with fear—

with heartbreak.

DJ staggered back up, blood dripping from his nose.

"Hold him—just hold—dammit, Caz—"

I thrashed violently, arms flinging out, nails scraping tile. Something primal took over—desperate, brutal. DJ grabbed my wrists and tried to force them down. I twisted, almost flipping him off entirely.

Caz snarled, "STOP FUCKING MOVING!"

But the killer was stronger than I ever knew I could be.

Stronger than I should've been.

For a moment, all three of us were locked in a tangled, shaking knot of grief, survival, and terror.

Then DJ found leverage.

He wedged his knee into my ribs, grabbed my arm, and slammed it behind my back.

Agony shot down my shoulder and I screamed—but it wasn't my voice.

I tried to say I'm sorry.

I tried to say thank you.

Nothing made it past my teeth.

Caz shifted her weight, driving her forearm deeper under my chin, pressing down, cutting off breath.

"Sleep," she gasped. "Just go to sleep, Russo—please—"

DJ gritted his teeth, tightening his grip.

"I've got him—Caz, I've got him—don't let go—"

My body jerked once.

Twice—

Then slowed.

Then collapsed.

The kitchen spun sideways.

Blood rushed in my ears.

My cheek hit the cold tile.

Somewhere far away, deep inside the dark, a voice whispered:

This isn't over.

And everything went black.

I woke to the feeling of motion.

The road hummed beneath me—steady, rhythmic, almost soothing. My vision swam as I blinked the blur away, head heavy, throat raw. For a moment, I didn't know where I was.

Then the metal bit into my wrists.

Handcuffs.

My hands were locked behind me.

I was in the backseat of DJ's car.

Darkness pressed in through the windows. Streetlights flickered across the interior in long, sickly gold streaks. Each pass of light sliced over DJ's profile—jaw clenched, eyes red, knuckles white on the steering wheel.

He didn't look at me.

Not once.

Caz sat in the passenger seat, turned half-away, hoodie pulled tight around her shoulders like she was freezing. Her hair was a mess, her cheek bruised, her eyes glassed over in a way I'd never seen.

She didn't look back either.

My voice barely made it out.

"...DJ?"

He shut his eyes. Just for a second.

Just long enough to ruin me.

"Niko," he managed, the word cracking in the middle.

Caz flinched when he said my name.

DJ swallowed hard, gripping the wheel tighter, the only thing keeping him from falling apart right there.

"I'm..."

The word died in his throat.

He tried again.

"I'm so sorry."

My chest caved inward.

There was blood dried on my clothes.

Rose's blood.

The memory slammed into me all at once.

I sucked in a breath like I was drowning.

"DJ—please—just—"

I didn't even know what I was asking for.

Forgiveness?

A chance?

A time machine?

None existed.

He shook his head without turning around.

"You're under arrest."

The words hit like a gunshot.

Caz closed her eyes, jaw trembling. She pressed her fingertips to her temple, trying not to cry—or trying not to scream.

DJ kept talking, voice barely steady:

"We're going to take you in. You're going to be processed. You're going to get help. And... and this stops tonight."

His voice cracked again.

"Niko, buddy... it has to."

Something inside me imploded.

The good part—the part that tried to fight it, save Rose, end everything before it got worse—that part curled inward and broke.

My forehead pressed against the window.

My breath fogged the glass.

And the city I once thought I was protecting slid by in silent streaks of orange and blue.

Caz finally spoke—quiet, brittle, nothing like her usual chaos.

"...Goodbye, Niko."

Not *see you soon.*

Not *hang in there.*

Not *we'll fix this.*

Just goodbye.

DJ turned the corner toward the precinct.

And the story ended exactly where it was always going:

Not with justice.

Not with closure.

But with the echo of a truth I never wanted to face:

I was here.

Now I'm not.

EPILOGUE

ONE WEEK LATER

They told me I'd been quieter lately.

The guards.

The doctor.

DJ—though he hadn't looked me in the eyes since that night.

I didn't talk much.

There wasn't anything left to say.

The world felt distant behind these concrete walls, like I was watching it through somebody else's dream. Time didn't move right here. It stretched and thinned and snapped back on itself. A week could be a day. A day could be a year.

They kept the lights bright.

They kept the doors locked.

They kept me alone.

But none of it kept *him* quiet.

The thing inside me.

The one who crawled up through the fractures in my skull.

The one who wore my voice when it wanted to.

The one who killed Dante.

Killed Toby.

Killed Maya.

Killed... Rose.

Sometimes I thought I heard him shifting under my ribs.

Whispering.

Laughing.

I sat on the edge of the cot, staring at the floor, when footsteps echoed down the corridor. Slow. Unhurried. Like someone savoring the sound.

Then a voice:

"Russo."

Caz.

I lifted my head.

She wore her leather jacket—ripped sleeve, peeling patches, one pin missing like she'd torn it off in a hurry. Her hair was up, messy, no space buns. Her eyes looked tired but bright in a way that felt... dangerous. And yes—her breasts were still impossible not to notice.

She stood just outside the bars.

"Hey," she said softly. Too softly. "You look... well. You look like shit, but also like you finally stopped fighting the universe."

I stared at her.

She stepped closer, fingers curling around the bars.

"You're not the same," she murmured. "Not even a little."

I didn't answer.

What was I supposed to say?

I wasn't the same.

I wasn't Niko.

I wasn't anything I recognized.

She studied my face like she saw both versions of me—the man she worked with and the creature that crawled out of him.

"Can I ask you something?" I finally managed, my voice scraping out like gravel.

"The red string... on Dante's finger. Why was it there? Why did you—"

Caz smiled.

A small, sharp, secret smile.

"Oh, Niko," she whispered, "I was wondering when you'd remember that."

She reached into her jacket pocket.

My pulse stuttered.

She pulled out a length of red string.

Bright.

Clean.

Untied.

She stepped up to the bars and held out her hand.

"Give me your finger."

My throat tightened.

But I lifted my hand anyway.

Slow.

Shaking.

She took my middle finger gently.

Her touch was warm.

And she wrapped the red string around it.

One loop.

Another.

A knot to hold it there.

"There," she said softly. "Now we match."

"...What does this mean, Caz?"

My voice barely made it out.

She inhaled—slow, deep—like she was savoring this.

"The truth," she said simply.

She leaned her forehead against the bars, eyes locked on mine.

"I loved Dante."

The world tilted.

My stomach dropped.

She kept going—quiet but steady, like she'd rehearsed it a thousand times.

"I was with him long before the department ever knew who he was. Before Tony started hunting him. Before Niko the Golden Boy swooped in to finish what his dad started. I kept him safe. Helped him disappear when cases got hot. Helped him hide the messier kills."

My breath stuck in my chest.

"But Dante..." She shrugged lightly. "He got sloppy. Soft. Rotted from the inside. His kills stopped meaning anything. They lost purpose."

Her eyes brightened.

"But you, Niko? You were blooming."

Something inside me twisted.

Tightened.

The killer stirred—warm and familiar.

"You didn't kill for chaos," she said. "You killed for

balance. For justice. You killed because the law failed you. Because the world took and took until something new had to rise up inside you to survive it."

I swallowed hard.

"Caz... what did you do?"

She smiled wider—a genuine, radiant smile that chilled me straight through.

She pulled a key from her pocket.

A cell key.

My heart stopped.

"Caz."

She fit the key into the lock.

For one stupid, fragile second, I thought about telling her not to.

Thought about staying.

Thought about Rose

But those thoughts couldn't stop my feet.

"It's time to go, Niko."

"No," I whispered. "I can't—"

She unlocked the door.

The mechanism clacked open, loud enough to echo through the block.

She stepped into my cell.

She cupped my jaw gently, thumb brushing the dried bruise there.

"You're not running from what you are anymore," she murmured. "I know you're scared. I know part of you still thinks you're the man you used to be."

The killer hummed behind my ribs.

Warm.

Awake.

She pressed her forehead to mine.

"But I've seen the real you. And I'm not letting you go to waste in here."

"Why?" I breathed.

She grinned like she was confessing a crush.

"Because, Niko... I don't have a thing for lost puppies or heroes."

Her hand slid down my arm, fingers brushing the red string.

"I have a thing for killers."

Her lips crashed into mine before I could react—and then she was pulling me out of the cell.

Footsteps echoed farther down the hall.

Guards on rounds.

She squeezed my hand.

"Come on."

And we ran.

Down the hall.

Past the shadows.

Past every place I thought my life ended.

Out a back door she'd wedged open twenty minutes earlier.

Into the night.

Into her car.

Into a future I should never have survived to see.

As the door slammed and the engine roared, Caz glanced at me, eyes wild and electric.

"One more thing," she said.

"What?"

She reached over and tapped the red string.
"You were never dead inside, Niko."
A grin—wicked, knowing—curved her lips.
"You were just becoming."
And we disappeared into the dark.

ACKNOWLEDGMENTS

Writing *He Was Here* was unlike anything I've done before. This book pushed me, challenged me, unsettled me, and changed me. It asked harder questions, dug deeper wounds, and demanded honesty from places I didn't always want to look. I could not have walked this road alone.

To Courtni—thank you for loving me through the chaos, the drafts, the late nights, the spirals, and every version of me that showed up along the way. Your patience, grounding, and belief in me carried this book through its darkest moments. I love you more than these pages could ever hold.

To my editor, Paige Lawson—you've sharpened my voice, strengthened my work, and helped shape this story into something sharper, tighter, and more haunting than I ever imagined. Thank you for every note, every push, and every moment you saw what this book could be before I did.

To my mom, who built a life for us from grit and faith—thank you for teaching me resilience, kindness, and the power of doing things scared. Your strength is in everything I write.

To my family and friends—everyone who has stood beside me on this wild author journey—your support means more than I can ever say. Thank you for cheering me on, even when the stories got dark, and for reminding me who I am outside the page.

To my daughters, Ellie, Emma, and Emelia—you are the brightest parts of every day. Your laughter and your love anchor me. This world, this work, this life... I do it all for you. I hope you always chase your wildest dreams.

To my ARC readers—thank you for returning, for believing in me a second time, for embracing the shift from AI-horror to serial killer thriller, and for meeting Niko Russo with the same intensity you met Evan Daniels. Your early reactions and support gave this book its heartbeat.

To my readers—old, new, returning, or curious— thank you for giving my stories a home. Thank you for trusting me with your time, your emotions, and your imagination. I never take that for granted.

This book is for anyone who's ever searched for justice when the world refused to hand it over.

For anyone who's carried anger heavy as bone.

For anyone who's felt like they were becoming something they didn't recognize.

You are not alone.

You are not broken.

And your story isn't finished.

ABOUT THE AUTHOR

ANTHONY MALLOY is an award-winning and bestselling author from Cincinnati, Ohio, where he lives with his partner, Courtni, and their three incredible daughters. His fiction was born in the fallout of a corporate layoff and carved itself into something sharper—stories that live where grief, identity, and obsession collide.

His debut novel, *Without You*, began as a late-night idea and evolved into a psychological thriller with teeth, redefining what he believed he was capable of. *He Was Here*, his second novel, digs even deeper into the darkness—exploring justice, guilt, and the monsters we become when the systems we trust break us instead of saving us.

When he's not writing, Anthony is a strategist, a story-teller, a pro wrestling fan, and a full-time dad. He believes in stories that hit hard, heal quietly, and refuse to be forgotten.

Stay connected with Anthony—visit his website for new releases, exclusive updates, and all the latest on his writing journey. You can also find him on Instagram and TikTok (@AnthonyMalloy.Author) or reach him by email at **contact@anthonymalloyauthor.com.**

instagram.com/AnthonyMalloy.Author

tiktok.com/@AnthonyMalloy.Author

goodreads.com/AnthonyMalloyAuthor

linkedin.com/in/AnthonyMalloy